Cosmic Decay Contamination

COURTNEY HOPE

ALSO BY COURTNEY HOPE:

Secrets of a Party Planner
Cosmic Decay: Contamination
Cosmic Decay: Debris

COMING SOON:

Cosmic Decay: Absolution

Courtney Hope is currently not represented by any publishing organisations. If you wish to represent Courtney, please visit www.courtneyhope.com.au

To *BYRON*

For all the love and support

And for watching way too many
horror movies with me.

PROLOGUE

In retrospect, their brash fascination with another world is what started it all.

Curious as to the human's psyche and jealous of the planet they inhabited, they needed to know why mankind was so different. As humans were contemplative of life's origins, and forever in search of the answers, they were no different in their questioning of existence.

Why are we here? What does it all mean?

As they collected their samples and analyzed their information, they started to realize that this inferior race called humanity could stand up to their science. While the humans weren't as advanced as they were, and certainly could never hope to be, there was still intelligent life among the destruction.

What made them decide to advance into this human world was the same egotistical trait that humans had. They saw themselves as the top of the food chain, the reason for their world's existence and progress. The Visitors knew that man's thought process was flawed.

It was humankind's constant search for intelligence and technology that was killing the earth. So many fumes, chemicals, unsafe construction and forest degradation were slowly destroying the beautiful planet they could never evolve to leave.

The Visitors knew how to advance the Earth without destroying it, and how to live with their much-advanced technology for millions of years before the planet began its natural order to crumble and decay away into the solar system. If the humans continued to exist in such a fruitless way, then the Visitors would have no choice but to accelerate the destruction and claim the resource as their own.

Following this reasoning, mankind certainly didn't deserve the world they evolved in, and that was why the Visitors decided to contaminate them, and take their beautiful world from them.

*****

Blue lights swam in front of his eyes, making him feel so cold and numb that he was paralyzed from it. A large head danced in and out of his vision, around the blue light. It was like no other head of any creature he had ever seen.

With what seemed like a thousand eyes searching the depths of his soul, Ian Peters could feel himself scream, but could not make any sound. The creature above him brought a giant metal scalpel with rotating nozzles closer to his body, and he could see a small vial of red oozing liquid seem to dance in the tube connected to the nozzle. He tried, unsuccessfully, to shriek and struggle.

Ian lifted his head with a jerk, knocking his half empty glass and a bowl of mixed nuts to the floor. He was caught off balance by his sudden movement and toppled off his bar room stool.

Lying on his back, Ian could hear laughter all around him as his vision swam. He tried to focus and bring his attention to the present to figure out where he was.

Once his vision stopped swimming, Ian could see the outline of the wooden bar that he had fallen away from and the cruel, twisted faces of other drunken patrons in the establishment as they stood around him, laughing. It dawned on him where he was and why everyone was laughing at him. Ian pushed himself to his elbows and then lifted himself up with all his strength. His body felt heavy as if it were made from bricks.

As he righted himself and picked up the toppled bar stool, Ian came to realize that the other patrons were still snickering at him.

Mr. McMason, a white-haired old oaf with teeth reminiscent of Stonehenge, came up to him, laughing so broad and hard that Ian was sure the old man would have a heart attack. McMason slapped him hard on the back of his right shoulder, causing Ian's whole body to shake from the unexpected strength.

"What's wrong, crazy?" McMason cackled, "Havin' another one of them whacked-out alien dreams?"

"Yeah, man!" piped up Tony Farrell by the pool table. "Your crazy ass story is legendary! What happened Peters? Did the little green men probe you a bit too hard?"

Tony's friends who were standing around the table with him all laughed maliciously, but Ian fell silent. He'd become used to this, but he sure was sick of it.

It was a story that was well known around his small hometown. Ian Peters was a used car salesperson, unhappy with the life that stuck him in a short-sleeved white business shirt and a too-tight tie that hung like a noose around his neck. Ian and his wife Rose used to fight a lot, and his stickybeak neighbor told all the other gossips in town. Many thought he was crazy or believed that he was suffering a very dramatic midlife crisis.

If only it had all been an elaborate prank, then maybe the nightmares wouldn't keep coming every time he shut his eyes.

Ian had been leaving work late one night after another gruelling shift of not selling any cars. He was walking to his beat-up steel trap when a large blinding blue light lit up the sky in front of him. It was all he could remember before waking up, in the darkness of a nearby field, owned by a small-town wheat farmer named Dog Johnson.

He had no idea what happened, but he groggily wandered the roads until a friendly face pulled up and offered him a lift. He didn't even remember the ride to his home, or who picked him up, but when he got there police cars were flashing their lights and lined up outside his house. Rose came running out of the house and over to him, collapsing into a surprisingly tear-filled bear hug.

Apparently, he had been missing for three days.

That was last night, and in coming home, Ian's story to the police had been spread about town by the gossipy neighbour. Ian had tried to fall asleep after returning home, but every time he did he dreamt of blue lights, heads with eyes that were as black and deep as space and red liquid that oozed in a series of small test tubes. He was so paralyzed with these night terrors that he was operating on no sleep.

It strained his relationship with Rose even more and made everything harder. Gone were the tears she wept for him the night he went 'missing'; the look in her eyes was now resentment and disgust at the mess her husband had become in such a short space of time.

His insomnia was so high that it had Ian dozing off in highly populated and unrestful places, like in the car yard earlier that afternoon and even in his local bar. He had obviously had one too many shots of bourbon to ease himself into going home and had drifted into a terrifying sleep.

Ian shook his head, feeling his blood starting to boil in anger. "It's a bit rich you calling me crazy McMason," Ian tried to reason, "You too Farrell. Shouldn't you be screwing your third ex-wife's daughter or something?"

That struck a nerve. Farrell stopped laughing and abruptly pushed off the pool table, sauntering over to Ian with a pool cue still in hand, ready to use it as a weapon.

"Oh, didn't you hear Ian?" Tony whispered angrily as he approached, the sound of his smooth voice making Ian's blood react even more to the sweaty closeness. "I've moved on from her. Now I'm having a poke at your old woman since you're too busy taking it up the ass by little green men to treat her right."

Tony's friends started to laugh again at the swing Tony had verbally made. Ian began to see physically red, as his blood reached boiling point. He began to concentrate on Tony's filthy, smiling mouth and imagined what it would look like to shove the whole pool cue he was holding.

"You can say what you want about me Farrell," Ian spat at him, "But don't you dare start stirring crap up about my wife!"

"And you know what Ian?" Tony continued to test him, "Boy, does that little piggy sure love to squeal!"

In a flash Ian was on Tony, tearing the pool cue from his hands and pushing him into the side of the pool table. Tony grunted at the impact, and the sudden hard shove sent the eight ball rolling away across the table. Ian snapped the pool cue against the table, splintering it into two pieces. Patrons with their drinks were springing into action, whether it was to move away from the fight or join in.

Ian raised the half broken pool cue to shoulder height and aimed its jagged broken edge at Tony's smug mouth. His mind only saw the red-hot rage brewing inside of him, and his eyes reflected it. Ian delighted at the look of terror reflected back at him through Tony's eyes.

Suddenly, hands were grabbing at Ian's arms, legs, and stomach, pulling him away from Tony. It was Farrell's three laughing friends, trying to protect their leader. They hung onto him as Ian struggled to break free.

Tony raised himself from the pool table, trying to regain his composure as Ian continued to struggle to charge at him like a bull at a matador.

"Hey, Ian! That's enough!" hollered the bartender from behind the bar. "Get the hell out of my bar Ian; I don't want to see you darkening that doorway ever again!"

"This was MY bar before it was ever his!" Ian angrily hissed, still kicking and fighting against Tony's friends.

"Well, it isn't anymore. It was one thing to have your crazy ass story follow you in here, and it's another to have you fall asleep all over the place, but damn it, Ian, enough is enough!" The bartender pointed to the front door, "Throw him out boys, and Ian if I hear you even so much as touch Tony Farrell for this I will tell the police, and you will be locked up in the crazy bin where you belong!"

Tony's friends lifted Ian up and took him, struggling, to the door where they set him down and gave him a hard push. Ian fell to the ground, cursing as he grazed his hands in the fall.

He turned around and shouted profanities as the three gave him one last menacing look before returning to their leader, slamming the door in Ian's face.

Ian muttered angrily as he scooped himself up off the bitumen. He hesitated and swayed where he stood, wondering what he should do and how he should get home. With his eyes seeing double as the combination of adrenaline and bourbon took hold, he decided he would leave his crappy car where it was parked outside the bar and walk the distance to his house to try and calm his nerves down. As he walked in the dark, his thoughts turned to the flashing blue lights and red oozing tubes, and instead of calming down he began to get more and more agitated. All he could feel was red, screaming hatred bubbling up inside of him and turning his world an even darker red than it was already.

Finally reaching home, Ian had been unable to soothe the feeling of hatred that started from the base of his cranium and had worked its way into popping a blood vessel in his eyeball. Why was he the one that the craziest kook in town called crazy? Why was he singled out that night coming home from the dealership? He had always paid his taxes on time, he didn't abuse Rose, and he didn't do hard drugs, so why was all this foul luck befalling him?

Walking up the path that led towards his front door, he kicked a rock a little too hard, and it smashed through the side windowpane next to the wooden door. Letting out a curse, Ian stopped and stared at the broken glass, shattered into a million little pieces like his very own life.

Suddenly, the porch light sprang on, and Rose angrily pulled open the door. Dressed in her pink nightgown with her sandy blonde hair cut short and hanging loosely at the base of her neck, she could have been so lovely if not for the ugly scowl on her face. In fact, for as long as Ian could remember, she always wore a scowl that darkened her features whenever he talked to her.

"What the hell did you do?" Rose yelled, looking down at the smashed windowpane. Ian made to go inside, but Rose pushed him back. "Have you been drinking at that damn bar again? Ian,

I can't handle this mindless destruction anymore!"

Ian felt his rage flare up again, and he stared Rose down, finally deciding to barrel past her to get into his home.

"I'll show you mindless destruction if you don't get the hell out of my way and let me into my damn house!" he snarled back at her, pushing her out of the way and stomping through the entrance corridor.

"And there you go again with the threats! I have had enough of you coming home smelling of bourbon, pushing me out of the way and treating me like part of the furniture!" Rose was yelling, but tears also started welling up in those hazel eyes. She spoke again, a bit more softly this time, "You never talk to me anymore, you never touch me. Not like before that day. At least when you were busy all the time and fighting with me, you spoke to me! I miss our fights, Ian, because at least you acknowledged my presence! Do you know how screwed up that is?"

Ian pushed open the fridge in the kitchen and pulled out a bottle of beer in the hope that it would help block the vile words looking to push their way out of this throat. He turned away from his wife and faced the kitchen window, trying not to look at the anguish on her face that no doubt mirrored his own.

"Well, good. At least we're fighting now! Are you happy? Maybe I wouldn't treat you like part of the furniture if you didn't treat my experience as an embarrassment, something to be laughed at!" he cried angrily.

"Ian, you claimed to be abducted by little green men!" Rose exclaimed, "Surely, you know how crazy you sound? I almost wished that you were having an affair and running around with a hussy for those damned three days! It would make this so much easier …"

"What so much easier?" Ian exclaimed as he turned back to face is wife.

"I'm leaving you, Ian," Rose told him, lowering her voice so that it was even. "I've met someone else. Someone more … stable. I can't handle this crazy spiral you have created for yourself and me sure as hell won't be dragged into it anymore."

Ian seethed. He knew exactly where this was going, or more precisely, who his wife was going to.

"It's Tony Farrell isn't it?" Ian demanded, his voice rising several octaves, imagining that devilish grin as he made fun of Ian in the bar. He knew it was true. Farrell was just too smug for his own good and too superior ever to keep a secret that he could throw in someone's face.

"He treats me better than you ever did. He's not afraid to make me feel again. I haven't felt anything but cold from you in a while," Rose snapped, her slow tears hardening on her cheeks.

Ian felt it again; that red-hot rage that had been bubbling up inside of him for a long time. He saw it through the red, Tony Farrell and his evil laugh as he proclaimed his smug affair with Rose at the bar while his hyena friends were laughing and throwing Ian onto the street. The images changed to Tony having his way with his wife—a place that Ian hadn't dared to go since the sudden existence of blinding blue lights in his life.

Ian's eyes and his mind were filled with a flash of brilliant colours: blackness as he tore the images from his mind, the blinding white light of an antibacterial haze, pulsating neon blue, and finally a flash of fiery red as his anger tore through his very existence. At the center of it all was Rose's defiant face and all the disbelief and hate she felt for him, and suddenly Ian mirrored her actions and her pain.

Smashing his beer bottle against the kitchen sink, Ian lunged for his wife. She screamed as he jumped on top of her in one swift action and cracked her smaller frame against the cupboard door, falling on top of her on the linoleum floor. Struggling underneath him, he saw the terror in Rose's eyes as she struggled to comprehend the reality of the situation. She knew that something had snapped and that this was the end. Before she could utter a single word to him, Ian raised what was left of his broken beer bottle and brought it down towards her neck, slicing the thin tissue there and ending the life of this woman he had once loved.

Rose's life force trickled out of her onto the linoleum, the blood oozing from the deep gash through her throat. Every one of Ian's tiny fibres and nerve endings jumped into action, like getting a jolt of electric energy from a large battery. He stooped down and ravished the wound in every conceivable manner—cutting, clawing, biting—destroying everything in a blinding red passion that was animalistic and primal.

Ian's fiery destruction flashed into a blinding white light, and he fell backward off the body of his wife, now lying silent and still except for the flow of her blood all over the kitchen floor.

The white-hot sensation in his mind sent tense spasms through his muscles, his skin, his organs—his very being. He felt the scarlet rage that became him flow through his body like his blood, but upon hitting the vital arteries in his heart, it became an electric blue calm that caused the pain and the anguish to subside and his vision to return. His body stopped twitching with adrenaline, and he lay there, out of breath, on the kitchen floor.

Once he had regained his strength, Ian pulled himself up off the floor and looked at the horrifying scene he had created. His lifeless wife's body was laid out in front of him, drenched in blood and looking unrecognizable where he had ravished it in a rage like that of an out-of-control pit bull. Blood had begun to congeal around the wounds and on the kitchen floor where it had flowed freely, and Ian realized that he too was covered in blood and grime. He had an overwhelming urge to get as far away from the body as possible, but staring at what was left of his wife Rose, he felt his mind begin to unravel.

What had he done? She was leaving him, but Rose never deserved to die over that. She should have left him long ago because she deserved much better. What had he become? Why was he even alive? What was this destructive rage that he had felt? He had never felt this angry in his entire life and Ian could just not comprehend what had come over him.

In the background, Ian could hear the wails of the police cars as they came closer to his neighbourhood. He realized that his fight with Rose and the sounds of her demise must have alerted his nosy neighbours to call the police, as they had done before when their fighting had become too much. Ian knew there was nothing left of him, and he deserved what he got, but he felt he couldn't face another human after destroying one in such an animalistic way.

Ian heaved himself towards the door that led to the backyard, his body stinging after the burst of adrenaline. The flashing lights of the police cars began to fill the room from the front of the house. With one last look at the proof of his destruction, Ian hurled himself out of the kitchen and out of the house, not fully realizing the extent of the damage that he had caused and the chain of events that he had put into motion.

The two police officers, a beautiful African woman named Tanya and a Caucasian man named Andy, came into the suburban home with their hands on their holstered guns. They had followed up on a domestic disturbance case at the Peters house before, as well as been on duty when the crazy Ian Peters went missing for three days earlier in the week, but they were surprised to discover the eerie silence that they walked in on. Usually, domestic cases filled the air with shouts and cries and broken furniture and tears. This was too quiet.

Tanya was the first to discover Rose in the kitchen. She was splayed out on the white linoleum that was stained red with her congealing blood. Rose was almost beyond recognition, gashed at the throat, but her head remained attached to her body by her damaged spine and some pieces of flesh at the back of her neck. Tanya yelled for Andy before she backed out of the room and called it in on her police radio.

Andy walked into the kitchen and cursed on site when he saw Rose Peters. He knew Ian, and he had always seemed a little nuts in thinking he had been abducted by aliens, but it seemed they now had proof that he had become completely unhinged, and unfortunately Rose Peters wasn't able to get out of the way in time. Andy knew that Rose was dead just by looking at her, and he decided to leave the body for the coroner and backed out of the room to find Tanya.

Andy reached Tanya in the hallway leading to the kitchen where she had just called in the murder. The cops at the station were no doubt scrambling together to get to the house while Tanya wished that she was somewhere else. Her hands wouldn't stop shaking as she re-holstered her walky-talky.

Suddenly, Andy heard a scraping and shuffling sound from behind him in the kitchen. Thinking it was perhaps a cat or a dog that the Peters had kept as a pet, he turned around to detain it and stop it from contaminating the body.

What he saw instead was no pet, but the strangest sight he had ever seen. It was so simply impossible that he felt paralyzed to move.

Rose Peters' corpse was standing up and staring straight at him.

Her head lolled to one side, arching backward and exposing the deep gashes and destruction in her throat that was barely holding her head to her body. Andy saw straight through it and knew that in every conceivable way she should not have been able to survive such a mauling and couldn't fathom what he was currently seeing.

Before Andy could utter a word, Rose's head slowly moved forward in his direction, making a horrible wet sound as it landed too far forward and lolled in place. Andy could see the tops of her eyes under the congealing blood and amongst the deadened hazel there was a startlingly bright supernatural ring of brilliant crimson around the iris.

In that second, the fragile corpse of Rose Peters became transformed in an animalistic rage and lunged for him, knocking Andy to the ground and pinning him there, surprisingly strong despite her slight frame and current physical condition. He felt her sticky blood flow from her wound onto him, and he could barely contain his disgust as he fell backward.

Rose Peters continued her attack on Andy, mauling and thrashing in a terrible frenzy that destroyed everything in her path like a dangerous and unpredictable hurricane. Tanya let out an ear-piercing scream from the hallway, and Rose turned what little she could of her head towards her, flashing her piercing now gray eyes and red irises in a hungry fashion.

Rose lurched off Andy—who had begun convulsing and was now laying silent in a mixed pool of blood and gore—and she dived towards Tanya. In her terror, Tanya's reaction time was off, and Rose brought her down quickly in a bloody attack against the wall.

Through her screams and the destruction, Tanya's vision swam fast, and she vaguely saw the body of her partner Andy spasm suddenly before he too got off the ground in a shuffling manner. The last thing that Tanya saw of her life was Andy's eyes as they mottled together to create the same gray pupils and red iris that engulfed Rose's own.

Slowly, in the silence and darkness, Tanya joined her fellow victims by convulsing spasmodically on the floor. In an instant, the change had come, and together, all three of them stood up amongst the debris of their attacks. They waited silently, their blood-soaked bodies practically crackling with raging energy, as the red and blue flashing lights of police sirens drew ever nearer to the end of the world.

Chapter 1

The world had decayed quickly in the five years it had taken for the rage-fuelled virus almost to wipe out the Earth's population. No one knew where it had come from, and soon there was hardly anyone left to wonder about it.

Cities had been reduced to ruins within a day, lives had been lost, governments had toppled, and the technology that had been the driving force behind innovation and evolution had failed them.

The basis of the virus seemed to stem from the very belly of the beast, and many survivors wondered if humankind's darker side had been the reason behind the sudden decay of the world. The evil and the greed, the dishonesty and senselessness had always existed in the core of human minds, and perhaps that had caused them to snarl and twist and feed on the hatred, to one day snap and pull everything that they loved into the abyss.

Perhaps that was where it all started; perhaps it was within mankind from the very beginning.

It wasn't long before nature took back what the humans had stolen from it. Tree roots cracked and destroyed concrete walls as if bursting through oppression. Plants grew within buildings, covering the walls with vines and the floors with moss. Animals were few and far between since their fight or flight senses caused them to flee or be killed, so mostly the nature-infested buildings and surrounding areas were silent.

Overrun concrete jungles were littered with debris. Buildings were blown out, walls crumbled and windows smashed. Blood stained the streets where possessions had fallen, and cars were overturned or were simply left abandoned, doors ajar. Shops were emptied, broken and looted, food supplies were low, and trivial items were scattered everywhere. It was the site of the apocalypse; the end of civilization.

And it had been snuffed out in one giant stampede.

*****

Walking among the ruin of a nearby city was a small scouting party made up of a man and a woman. Max Stone was a chiselled man, with short blonde hair and beautiful blue eyes that had seen much terror and heartache. His goal was to make it through this new world and protect his wife; the woman also in the scouting party. He wore gray cargo pants, a gray t-shirt, and a black cargo jacket. Around his waist was a gun belt that holstered a pistol and some extra rounds, while slung on his back was a black backpack bulging with food and other supplies.

The woman, Victoria Stone, was a determined brunette with golden brown eyes and a curvy figure. She wore a pair of dark pants, a brown leather jacket and big brown boots with a solid heel and steel-capped toes. She carried her own pair of pistols that were holstered in two matching gun belts tied around her thighs and carried a small, manual chainsaw slung to her back like a backpack. Signs of blood long since shed were splattered all over the blades.

The couple that slays together stays together, and these two were inseparable. Their love had become their own beacon of hope in this cold gray world.

Snaking in and out between buildings and wreckage, Max and

Victoria kept low to the ground and as quiet as possible so that they didn't enrage the Mindless that now aimlessly roamed the streets, looking for something to eat.

They weren't far from their destination, a tall white block of apartments where the others in their hunting party were situated. They had cleared out the whole apartment block of the Mindless tenants who used to live there and created a floor for the still living. It was flush with canned goods, torches, ammunition, weapons and other survival gear. Each outside patio had been equipped with sniper rifles that were mounted on stands and ready to go should members of the new Mindless community approach the apartment block.

The large white row of apartments was situated only one intersection away from the sizeable shopping mall that was once the bustling focus for busy shoppers. Snaking around the farther side of the mall was a generous, once beautifully cared for lake that was now home to slimy green algae and overgrown reeds. The lake flowed around a series of buildings that overlooked a grassy courtyard directly across from the mall. It was an excellent location because every week Max and Victoria conducted scouting missions to the nearby mall, where they looted everything they needed to keep surviving in the decaying rubble.

After stocking up on everything they could find, Max and Victoria were coming back to their home with emptier pockets than usual. The mall had finally been wiped clean of all the important ingredients and now had nothing left to use in it but rotted material possessions and rancid dairy and meat products. All fridges and freezers, shelves and back rooms had been overturned in the search for necessary survival items, and Max and Victoria were not the first ones to have ravaged it since the destruction of the local human race. They would have to travel a little further next time, and without being within reach of their makeshift gun turrets on the balconies of the apartment, it might be a little harder to get home.

A dishevelled Mindless man ambled passed them in the middle of the road, and they took their chance to round the corner of the cement building they were hiding behind. Max and Victoria dropped behind a low wall separating the sidewalk from the row of wrecked and burnt out cafes that lined the street. They crawled like commandos behind the wall, trying not to make any sound so that the Mindless was not alerted to their presence.

He was already curious, turning towards their direction when he saw a flash of brown out the corner of his cold, gray eyes.

Max and Victoria had almost made it to the end of the wall and were preparing themselves for the next quick dash behind a burnt out shell of a sedan when Victoria accidentally crunched some glass under her steel-capped boots. She held a sharp intake of breath as she waited to hear if the Mindless had heard the sound as well. Max quickly peeked out from behind the wall, in the hope of seeing nothing but it's putrefying back as it shuffled away.

They weren't that lucky; it had heard everything. It's red irises bulged as it caught sight of Max's head and starting running towards them.

"Go!" Max shouted, rising to his feet and pulling Victoria up with him. Together the two of them started for the apartment, running as fast as they could. In through the nose and out through the mouth, their breath was caught in ragged gasps as they ran towards their home.

Max sneaked a peak behind him and saw that the Mindless was almost upon them. Damn, they were some fast runners once the adrenaline kicked in! The Mindless were generally slow, shuffling creatures, but once they became alerted to their next meal the adrenaline-driven rage gave them a velocity and ferocious strength that could take them over great distances, fast. The creature let out an enraged screeching sound that Max knew would alert others in the area, and he was aware that it had to be silenced.

"Victoria! Go for it!" he cried, and he watched her slow down until he had passed her. He turned and pulled his pistol out, aiming directly for the head of the Mindless, should he not go down quickly at the hand of his wife's deadliest weapon.

Victoria reached her hands over her shoulder and pulled her chainsaw from its pouch on her back until she was holding it in both hands. In one fluid movement, she pulled the cord and roared the soft manual motor into life. The Mindless was now almost upon her, and she continued to wait with her hands on her slightly vibrating weapon. As the Mindless came within attacking distance, Victoria pierced the blade of the chainsaw through its stomach, like a hot knife through melting butter.

Blood and intestines splattered everywhere as the Mindless still reached for her—its hands almost closing in on her before the top half fell apart from its bottom half. It landed with a hard thud on the ground.

The Mindless one's lower torso had kept running and smacked straight into Victoria. She bent backward slightly and positioned her boot on it, kicking it to the curb before she stomped over to the upper torso and stood before the still-struggling upper body of the Mindless. Without compassion, Victoria laid the chainsaw into its skull. The Mindless' gray eyes bulged, and its mouth opened and screeched, congealed blood pooling out. Once Victoria had destroyed the brain, the lifeless body stopped twitching, and she pulled her bloody saw from what was left of the head, stopping the blade with a flick of a switch.

Gasping for breath after her own adrenaline surge, Victoria looked up from over the Mindless one's body and saw four more running up the road near the lake. She cursed under her breath before she flung the bloody chainsaw back into the pouch on her back, and she and Max took off once more.

They had the advantage of distance, but the Mindless had the advantage of extra adrenaline pulsing in their lifeless veins. They were picking up speed and gaining on the couple.

Victoria and Max ran at full speed across the street and flung themselves at the stairs that led to their apartment complex. Victoria looked over the banister and saw that the Mindless were gaining on them, so they took the stairs almost four at a time to try and increase the space between them.

They rounded the corner and saw a Mindless turn towards them from the middle of their path, unaware of the daring chase that had been happening on the street behind it. Max aimed his pistol at its head and fired off a shot that embedded itself into its rotting brain. It fell into its final death as Victoria and Max jumped over it to continue up the stairs behind it.

Gunfire and noise generally brought more of them, but with four of the Mindless on their tail and a Mindless in their way, Max hadn't had much of a choice in firing off his gun.

Victoria and Max made it up the stairs and bolted through the courtyard towards their apartment building, but the four Mindless creatures were close behind them, narrowing the distance. Victoria could see the panelled-up door of the apartment ahead of her and prayed that this scouting mission wouldn't be their last.

Four rounds from a sniper rifle popped off from above them and hit all four of the chasing Mindless squarely in the head. They fell where they were, face first carried forward by the momentum of their running, littering the courtyard.

Victoria and Max slowed as they reached the armoured gate of the apartment building, which had been constructed out of heavy metal and wood. The survivors who had been holed up in here couldn't guarantee that the Mindless couldn't break into the bottom apartments, so they had built a cement wall in the main hall of the building, separating the other apartments from the sealed lobby. They had constructed the gate with a metal peephole to help provide extra protection for their new little center of the world.

The man at the gate, a nervous looking man named Ian Peters, was breathing heavily as he opened the door and hurriedly let them in. Victoria and Max panted and tried to catch their breath as Ian nervously took in Victoria's blood-stained outfit.

"You didn't get bitten anywhere, did you?" He asked quickly, looking her up and down. He was always concerned about ways to catch the virus. "You didn't get any in your mouth or eyes?"

"No Ian," Victoria panted, annoyed that he asked them this question every time they came back from a scouting mission. He must have been a doctor or something because he always tried to check them over, scared of what he would find and what they could bring back into their secure facility.

"Well, you can never be too careful you know! I've seen people turn through bites and wounds and, and ..." Ian trailed off, his mind obviously reliving its own version of Hell.

"We know Ian, don't get bitten or scratched. We didn't. It's fine," Max told him in that hard but reassuring voice of his, cutting Ian off from continuing down his worrying spiral. He thumped Ian reassuringly on the shoulder and pulled Victoria towards the fire door, leaving Ian downstairs to make sure the door was fully closed and armed for the night.

"Geez, he asks that every time," Victoria breathed as they walked up the six flights of stairs, annoyed at Ian's persistence.

"He's just careful Victoria. Have you seen your outfit? No wonder he's worried you got some in your mouth. You look terrible!" Max joked.

Victoria took herself in. She had blood and guts all over her t-shirt and leather jacket, as well as a leaking stain from the pouch on her back that held her used chainsaw. She cursed under her breath and looked at Max as they climbed the stairs.

"Damn … I liked this outfit too. It's going to take ages to get the blood out of the leather."

"It's a good thing that red is in this season," Max joked, and Victoria giggled. He always made her laugh, even in these troubled times.

"You did well with the chainsaw honey," Max told her, returning to a more serious mood. Victoria smiled.

"I always do well with the chainsaw. Nice shot with the Mindless on the stairs, by the way," Max nodded at her compliment. It was always nice to praise and appreciate each other. It was one of the keys to a successful marriage, even in trying times.

They reached the sixth floor and pushed open the fire door.

They could smell food cooking as they walked down the hallway. The door to apartment fifty-one opened and a skinny, but lean, guy with black hair tied back into a ponytail and long stubble peeked out.

"Nice shot Jay!" Max complimented, as he smacked his hand in a sort of secret guy handshake. Jay Welles emerged from the apartment with a silenced sniper rifle in his hand, having been the one to shoot at the four Mindless creatures that had just been chasing them.

"Thanks, man!" Jay said to Max, following them up the hall to the end apartment. "Danny is still out there picking off the stragglers that were alerted to the action, but it's looking quiet now."

The three of them reached the end of the hall where an apartment had been opened up into a common area. A few people were milling around, eager to see what Victoria and Max had brought.

Besides Ian, Jay and Jay's friend Danny Masters, Victoria and Max shared their little apartment area with a few other people.

There was a tall African woman with curly brown hair named Jacinta Reinhart, who had a hard exterior and was tough in the field. She always wore her armour, physically and emotionally, and it was tough to crack. Besides Jacinta, there was a Mexican family who didn't speak a lot of English, but were nice enough people who were hard workers and experts in agriculture, growing different fruits and vegetables on the balcony of their own apartment. The family was made up of the father, a roundish man with a moustache named Hulio Flores, a curvy, round mother named Diana, and two young children by the names of Alejandra and Jose.

Besides them, there was a fourteen-year-old, wide-eyed girl named Mia Cavallari, who had lost everyone she had cared about pretty recently. Her whole family had been holed up just outside of the city when the world had been overrun; when the Mindless had finally reached them, she lost everyone trying to escape. She was tough about it, but her eyes still reflected the sadness she felt within her heart.

The whole group eventually came out to meet Victoria and Max in their communal area, and Diana stopped cooking the meal she was preparing on a camping stove. Max swung his backpack off his shoulders and pulled out the supplies they had scavenged from the mall.

"Unfortunately, we don't have much—the mall has been completely taken in regards to food, so we're going to have to spread out further for more supplies," Max told the group, pulling out the cans of beans and corn they had collected. "If we eat what we have it will last another couple of days and then we will have to go out on another scouting mission, but it will be further from home, and we will need more people for that."

The group nodded in agreement before they started putting the cans away. They had developed a system which meant that the entire group shared the items that were scavenged throughout their many scouting trips and that they had large communal meals in the common area to ensure they all received equal portions and equal parts of the rations.

Victoria caught Alejandra checking out her blood-stained outfit, and she decided to make her exit. "I'm going to the third floor to start cleaning myself up. I'll meet you guys back up here for dinner."

Victoria turned and started heading down the corridor to the third floor, where Hulio and the group had rigged up the plumbing so that they could at least get access to some water to clean themselves and their clothes.

Max watched Victoria go, especially the sway of her curvy hips as she headed down the corridor. He loved his wife very much and appreciated her beauty every day. In a world that had been darkened with pain and anguish and horror, it was sometimes hard to find a bright spark that lit up the shadowy corners, but he found it regularly in Victoria.

He started thinking about their relationship, and how better they felt to be safe and in a home that had others around for added protection. It meant that they could finally be comfortable and intimate, despite the despair that daily seeped in through the windows. They had been through enough.

"I'll be back guys," Max murmured to the group and followed Victoria down the corridor, practically running to catch up to her. He caught Jay's attention on his way out and Jay wiggled his eyebrows at him as he ran past. Max could hardly catch the grin that was leaking out.

Sometimes, with the world the way that it was, it was hard to grin. But in this particular instant, with the love of his wife, he could. He deserved to be happy once in a while. They all did.

Chapter 2

Victoria sat on the balcony of the apartment that she shared with Max with the morning sun glowing brightly in the sky and lighting up the decay around her. She was dressed in nothing but her underwear and a slightly oversized pink t-shirt that reminded her of younger, better days. Her hair was tousled slightly from sleep, and as she sat on the tiled floor in front of a washboard and bucket of water, she tried to get the bloodstains off of her jacket.

She felt like everything was back to normal and like she was a newlywed again. Her mind flashed back to the night before when she and Max had been permitted to have a rare moment of intimacy and happiness in this decaying world. She smiled cheekily to her-self as she thought of Max in the shower, with the cold soapy water from the camping shower running down his hardened naked body. Pressing her own naked, slippery body against him created a spark that was just bright enough to rekindle the electricity that was continually being challenged in this darkened world.

Despite the problems she and her little group encountered regularly, it was nice to have someone to love and something to live for. Many people just couldn't cope with their loved ones succumbed to the curse that was the Mindless, and committed suicide when the plague started taking shape. They had simply given up hope. The most disappointing had been the masses that had just wanted to be a part of the crowd and couldn't stand the fight. But for Victoria, she and Max had gotten through it with their strength and their resilience—and for each other.

It was nice to have a reason to keep living and surviving like she did with Max. He was the source of her strength, and she would do anything for him. It was why they went on raids together. They knew what the other was going to do before they did it, without even having to discuss the situation. Their connection was just that deep that they could practically read each other's minds.

It was handy whenever they were facing down a horde. They knew that their connection gave them the best chance to get out every time, no matter what.

The breeze rustled softly through the mounds of concrete that was their little white apartment complex, dragging with its stifled moans from the streets below. Occasionally, the Mindless would come into the courtyard at the apartment, but because Hulio and Diana were the current lookouts and were waiting with silenced sniper rifles at their own balcony, Victoria felt as safe as she possibly could feel.

She didn't expect the sudden change when it came.

The breeze turned into stronger gusts of wind without warning and started to pick up speed and force. In an instant, it became gale force with the strength of a hurricane behind it. Victoria's jacket fluttered vigorously against the wind, and she had to hold her hands to her face so that her eyes weren't stung by the dust that was suddenly billowing from the ground. The windows rattled in the apartment behind her, and she saw small pieces of debris take flight in the driving wind, moving past the building.

The world around Victoria was suddenly filled with a high pitched shrieking sound that forced her to move her hands to her ears and squeezes her eyes shut, trying to keep out both the wind and the horrible sound. She had heard shouts from behind her from her group in their own apartments before their voices were carried away quickly by the wind.

She felt a strong hand grab her by the shoulder, and she knew it was Max. She grabbed her jacket and got up, following Max's arm, unseeing as she braced herself against the wind and the horrifying sound that was still shrieking in her ears. The tin wash bucket and board she had been using quickly toppled over, splashing soapy water over the tile floor of the balcony. The pair were forced to the side of the building by the power of the wind and groped for the glass guard railing.

Victoria was led blindly by Max into their apartment building where he struggled to shut the door against the wind. Victoria reached out to find a wall to lean on, dropping her jacket before trying to wipe the dirt and dust out of her eyes. The windows shook and somewhere she heard a loud bang and a shatter.

"What's going on?" Victoria questioned, rubbing the last of the dust from her eyes and pushing herself off the wall. She turned around to face the window and saw that Max was standing quite still, looking outside the windowed door with his back to her.

The wind had settled down, and returned to the light breeze it had once been when Victoria was sitting on the balcony. She crossed to join Max and looked out of the win-dow but couldn't see past the glass railing where the bucket and washboard were now wedged. To get a better look past the cloud of dust still spiralling in the breeze, Victoria carefully opened the door and tiptoed quietly onto the balcony.

It was apparent that in that fleeting few moments everything had changed. The air was stale and had an almost electric quality about it like a lighting storm had just struck. The dust storm that stung Victoria's eyes was filled with a shrill hum of machinery.

The morning glow had disappeared and was replaced with a pale blue light that pulsed with eeriness and cut through the rusty hue of the air.

The light was emanating from a large oval-shaped metallic ship that had landed in the middle of the intersection between the apartment building and the mall—right where Victoria had used her chainsaw on the Mindless man the day before. The craft was futuristic in design, with many tubes, pipes, and glowing parts lighting up the sides that they could see. The air shimmered under it, propelled by an unearthly gas fuming from the tubes and pipes that lined it. The gas met with glowing hot lightning rods that were lowering the ship to the ground. They each gave a small explosive burst that completely decimated the ground directly underneath the landing zone, causing the concrete to seemingly come apart like waves on a shoreline and making a large hole in concrete and earth for the metallic ship to land completely in, like some giant prehistoric bird settling onto its nest

Max appeared beside Victoria on the balcony and looked out in shock. Large holes in the ship began to open, peeling themselves away like a cut in solid tissue, making a grinding noise as they did so. The opening process was slow moving but oddly took no time at all. The amount of metallic, gaping holes that opened along the side of the ship was in the hundreds.

Max and Victoria gasped in horror as they watched a mass of slimy indistinguishable body parts slide out from the holes and land with a careful splat on the ground. The bodies seemed to melt together with silvery mucus that covered the different parts, growing into a hulking torso with large shoulders and arms, thick legs, and a large oval-shaped head with an enormous cranium. Once reassembled, the creature stood up on its hind legs, looking almost Jurassic. It opened a hole at the bottom of a snout like part on its head and let out a deafening screeching; a sound that caused Max and Victoria to involuntarily cover their ears.

Somewhere behind them, in their sixth-floor apartment complex, screams were emanating. Victoria and Max could do nothing but watch on in horror as these Visitors from another world squirmed into life and turned their attention to the large group of Mindless, who had been alerted to their presence, possessing just enough life to see a meal in these new additions to their menu.

The Mindless moved as a group, running together like the crest of a wave to attack the Visitors, who continued to drop from the holes and form their celestial bodies around the massive ship. Max and Victoria watched a Mindless man gather speed and reach one of the Visitors, before a flash of brilliant blue light completely decimated both him and the smaller swarm that was close behind him.

Suddenly, the world seemed to flash in a series of blinding blue lights and blurs as the Visitors were alerted to the presence of the Mindless and took absolutely no pause or concern in destroying each and every one of them. Bodies ripped apart at the seams and splayed themselves around the intersection; staining every last area except the Visitors and their ship with blood and decay. The sound of this decimation was a metallic screech that filled the air and was followed by absolute silence.

Unable to move away from the horror show, Victoria watched as the Visitors harnessed what seemed to be the cause of the pulsing blue devastation—a long metallic gun that attached itself to the large wrist of the creatures. Slowly the Visitors surveyed the surrounding areas for Mindless stragglers before jumping into action. They used their powerful hind legs to quickly cover a large amount of terrain and spread out, branching off in all directions.

Max and Victoria quickly ducked behind the cement wall of their balcony as one seemed to turn it's elongated cranium in the direction of their apartment building. With their back to the outside world, they spotted Mia opening the door of their apartment and running to the glass door in a panic.

"You have to help!" she cried, "Ian is freaking out. Did you see what they did to the Mindless? He is screaming and is going to give us away. We will end up just like them if he doesn't stop! You have to do something!"

Max and Victoria jumped up from their hiding spot and ran into the building. Victoria paused to quickly pull on a pair of jeans and grab her manual chainsaw from its home beside the front door before following them out to the communal area.

Ian was huddled in a ball against the kitchen cupboards, rocking slowly back and forth. His face showed nothing but sheer panic and he wouldn't—or couldn't—stop muttering loudly to himself. Diana and Hulio stood around him, clutching their terrified children to their bodies.

"They've come to get us and finish the job. They've come for us. This is it! It's all over. Don't let them get me, don't let them get me," he turned to Max, who was standing over him. "Don't let them get me again!" he cried, pulling his head into his arms to continue his muttering.

"Ian, you need to be quiet now," Max told him in a firm voice as Victoria knelt down next to him and put her chainsaw behind her, just out of his reach, should he decide to do anything drastic.

"What do you mean they have come to finish the job?" Mia asked, concerned with this new idea of how the world had ended. "What do you mean "again"? What do you know Ian?!"

"It's my fault!" Ian sobbed, hiding his face from the group in his hands. "I started this. I … I … they took me! Blue lights … their heads in front of me, and then red … red everywhere!"

Ian peeked out from underneath his hands and looked Victoria straight in the eyes, kneeling down in front of him. Victoria let out a gasp of shock when she saw Ian's eyes—tear streaked and horrified as they were—reflect the same red ringed iris that was a common trait in the Mindless.

But it was different—ringed around the red was another small ring of electric blue. It was like nothing she had ever seen before, unlike any of the humans or the Mindless had ever displayed.

"It's my fault!" He told her again, "They put something in me … a curse. Something red and bubbling. I killed my wife. I didn't mean to, I didn't want to … but everything was red, and I killed her. And then she came back … I saw it, from the neighbour's yard! She came back and killed everyone else … and then they came back. And now the world is this way, and it's all my fault, and now they have come to finish the job!"

Ian hid his eyes again and began to rock back and forth muttering, squealing a little too loudly. The group stood around him, frozen in horror at his story. Could it have been true? Were these mysterious Visitors the reason behind the world's destruction?

"If this was your fault, Ian, then why aren't you infected like everyone else out there?" Mia asked quietly, clearly terrified.

"I don't know …" Ian said in a voice so soft they could barely make out the words, "I've always been immune … here now to take me away."

"Guys …" Victoria said in a warning tone from her kneeling position next to Ian. She slowly and quietly directed their eyes to Ian's shirt, which was untucked and torn slightly in places from being overworn. She lifted the shirt up slightly and showed the group what she had just now caught sight of—about six bite- and scratch-shaped scars marked the skin on Ian's back. Each mark was deep and raw and not well tended to, with rough stitches poking out and swelling dotting the lines on his skin.

Under each mark, was a bruise, but they were not a purple colour, or yellow, as a normal bruise would turn when fading away; each bruise was a bright blue colour pulsing under his pale skin.

Ian had been bitten and attacked by the Mindless many times, but had survived each bite and had never turned.

Ian Peters truly was immune. He was victim zero.

"Uh, guys!" Jay ran from the sliding glass door of the balcony in the communal area, "I hate to tell you this, but we've got one of them looking in the apartments across the road. I hate to say he's right but they are looking for something, and I guess it's not just the Mindless they tore apart on the street."

Danny and Jacinta moved in behind him, backing away from the window with their guns raised and weapons at the ready.

"Ian's too loud," Danny whispered. "We don't know anything about them. They could have super sensitive hearing."

Victoria saw the panicked look in Mia's eyes and the way Danny and Jay were backing away from the balcony with worried expressions. They were right. She turned to Ian huddled in the kitchen and put an arm around his shoulders.

"Ian honey, we need you to be quiet now," Victoria told him in her most soothing voice.

Ian's shaking got worse, and his voice only got louder "Coming closer now. Coming to take everything else. I CAN'T DO IT ANYMORE! I CAN'T DO IT!" he shouted suddenly.

Max looked out the window and saw the Visitor turn its massive head in the direction of their apartments, blinking the dark holey pit that was its eyes. It had climbed up the sidewall of the next apartment block like a spider. Max knew that if Ian didn't stop, he would actually pinpoint their presence to the Visitors, and that would end their lives. Max didn't want it to end like this, not after all the determination and planning it had taken to survive this long at the hands of the Mindless, and not after everything they had been through.

Max bent down until he was face to face with Ian, who turned his head towards him. Ian's eyes were haunted with the past and terrified of the future, but Max too saw that his irises were ringed in the red animalistic curse of the Mindless, and in an electric blue as well. Without warning, Max punched him square across the cheek, knocking him out instantly and forcing him to fall into Victoria's waiting lap. Mia, standing beside them, was shocked at the sudden brutality, but remained silent except for the small gasp that escaped her lips.

"Everybody hide! Now! Anywhere and do anything to avoid being seen!" Max barked as softly as he could. Instantly everyone in the communal area scattered, looking for their own hiding spots.

Max picked Ian up by the waist and dropped him roughly over his broad shoulders. Victoria rose from her place on the kitchen floor, grabbing her chainsaw. She and Mia followed Max as he carried Ian out of the kitchen and into the first apartment he could find, which happened to be Diana's and Hulio's.

Victoria looked back and saw the Mexican couple packing Alejandra and Jose into the kitchen cupboards of the communal area while Jacinta ran off with Jay and Danny into their own apartment, armed with guns and kitchen knives.

Kicking open the door, Max beckoned the girls to follow him into the bedroom. He moved in and roughly dropped Ian to the floor, pushing him under the bed.

"Get under with him," Max instructed Mia. "If he wakes up tell him to stay quiet. Whatever you do, don't move. Victoria and I will be right here."

Mia nodded and slid in under the bed with Ian. Max and Victoria opened the sliding mirrored cupboard opposite the bed and climbed into the small area amongst Hulio and Diana's tiny collection of worldly possessions. Victoria, who was the closest to the door, held her chainsaw in her hands at the ready and left the cupboard door open an inch so that they could see out into the bedroom.

In and out, Victoria's quickened breath slowed as she tried to get it under control to avoid making a lot of noise. She heard some glass shattering in the communal area and some soft slithering and shuffling sounds that alerted her to the fact that the Visitors had breached the secure perimeter of the apartment building. There were no screams or sounds of a violent attack, so it was safe to assume that Hulio, Diana, and their children had not been found in the kitchen.

A harsh wooden ripping sound vibrated closely around them, and they realized that the Visitor was following them into Diana and Hulio's apartment, ripping the closed door off its hinges. The shuffling sounds came closer as it was obviously making its way through the different rooms. Had it seen them come in here?

The Visitor came into view from their hiding spot causing Victoria to stifle her urge to scream. It was the ugliest thing she had ever seen, and she had seen many beheaded and limbless Mindless. They had once been human and were built as she was, so the horrific destruction of humanlike bodies was an ugly sight in itself.

The skin of the Visitors seemed like a mass of dark mottled rope, wound together to create their hulking bodies. It was like seeing a decayed and mummified body up close, back when museums used to house exhibits for tourists.

Their skin stretched over their large craniums, and their mouths were nothing but dark, twisted holes protruding in a rounded muzzle shape. They had large black eyes that were set wide apart on their large heads. The dark holes seemed to be everywhere, sinking down into the depths of Hell without an end.

Victoria saw the Visitor's dark eyes bulge and grow illuminated blue rings around the area where an iris would be— the same electric blue that had been surrounding the red in Ian's eyes. The startling blue was the only light emanating from the whole creature. The Visitor's hulking body stalked towards the bed, and she knew in an instant it was going to find Ian and Mia.

It reached its long ropey arms under the bed and splayed its three suction-capped fingers out on the end of it.

Horror mounted in Victoria's chest as the Visitor wrapped its fingers around Ian's ankle and pulled the man out, still unconscious from Max's punch. She heard Mia shuffle as she tried to hold on to Ian without being seen, but the Visitor pulled his whole body out without any resistance and held him up in the air by the left ankle. Ian's body was limp and dangling in its unconscious state, with a bruise starting to swell around his closed eyes.

As the Visitor's eyes continued to glow a brilliant pulsing blue, energy and adrenaline seemed to seep from Victoria's pores and from her very being. She and Max had worked so hard to keep everyone together and to keep everyone safe. Ian had just revealed something that could be extremely prevalent to the survival of humankind.

She couldn't let it end now.

Max felt it when she did and reached out to stop her, but Victoria was already pushing the sliding door open and springing from the cupboard, roaring her chainsaw to life with one easy pull of the cord. In one movement, contained within the Visitor's split second of surprise, she brought the blade of her chainsaw through the thick arm that held onto Ian. The blade pulsed through the Visitor's thick meat, threatening to lodge and come to a standstill, but with all of Victoria's might, she pushed the rotating and whirring blade in deeper. Purple blood spurted everywhere as the chainsaw finally cut through the thick tissue, and the arm fell to the bed, flopping the unconscious Ian there too.

Victoria's chainsaw had whirred for another few seconds before it sputtered out and she looked up into the eyes of the beast, suddenly afraid of her actions. The Visitor turned its steely dark gaze on her and filled its eyes with the brilliant illustrious blue that had rimmed its irises.

With a scream that Victoria vaguely realized was hers, she was frozen, unable to move and unable to fight. All the strength and power was instantly drained from her as she stared trance-like into the Visitor's pulsing eyes that were as a deep and dark as a well.

Max jumped out of the cupboard and pulled his gun from the waistband of his jeans. In that same instant, the creature looked down at its missing arm, where thick mucus had formed around the bleeding gash. Suddenly, an arm burst from the purple mess where it's old one had been and spurted leftover slime and blood onto the gray carpet of the bedroom floor.

The Visitor flexed its new arm muscles and grabbed both its arm and Ian from the bed, slinging them both over its broad shoulder. It turned and stared again at Victoria with its glowing blue eyes and she continued to remain still, full of the shock and with a supernatural hold on her. The Visitor looked at the arm that was detached from its body and then back at Victoria, obviously angry that she had been the one to take it. It opened its gaping mouth wide and let out a shrill scream that pierced into everybody's ears. Max doubled over in pain, trying to think of a way to release Victoria from the thrall of the beast, but all of his brain power was compelled to retreat as it was pierced with the Visitor's screech.

The loud shrieking noise caused the window behind the Visitor to shatter into a million pieces, splintering around the Visitor, avoiding hitting it square in the back, and instead raining over the entrance. The Visitor let out another screech before using its long, thick legs to shoot backward, propelling itself, the unconscious Ian dangling over its shoulder, and pulling the silent Victoria out along with it.

"No!" Max screamed through the noise and made for the shattered window. He jumped out onto the balcony that ran the length of the apartment and ran to the glass railing, looking over. He watched helplessly as the Visitor used its long legs and suctioned cup toes to navigate down the side of the building while holding Victoria in one hand, and with Ian and its detached arm slung over its meaty shoulder.

Mia crawled out from under the bed with tears in her eyes, jumped through the glassless window and stood next to Max, watching the Visitor carry Ian and Victoria away.

"What do we do now?" she asked in a terrified tone, looking to her once fearless leader. Max now held a look of complete devastation on his face. His whole world had been ripped away from him, and he had absolutely no idea what to do about it.

CHAPTER 3

Victoria's vision came in a bright blue haze. She vaguely recognized that she was walking, and she was aware that she was following a large hulking torso and the unconscious body of Ian. Victoria's world hadn't grown dim but had, in fact, become a source of brilliant colour. The world was illuminated in a shade of white so bright that her mind couldn't comprehend it. She felt herself moving at a pace and a time that was not her own and she couldn't force herself to stop.

In her brilliant white vision, Victoria saw a flash of dark gray run into the massive moving rope of muscles that was the Visitor and bite straight into its meaty shoulder. She saw the Visitor spring into action, caught unaware by its attacker as it let out a piercing shrill that vibrated through her haze.

Victoria suddenly felt the Visitor's pain deep inside her very core, pulsating through the brilliant light. It reverberated within her and as she blinked against the bright hues she vaguely noticed the Visitor was writhing around, tearing wildly at a small bloody mass attached to its back.

Another shrill, high-pitched scream came from the Visitor and was followed by sudden darkness; Victoria feared she was suddenly blind. To combat the darkness, she forced her eyes opened and realized groggily that she was lying on her back. She blinked in the normal sunlight and tried to readjust her vision and get the feeling back into her body, which was now suddenly her own again. Her heart rate began to quicken the sluggish pace it had taken on under the spell of the Visitor, as she worked her muscles which slowly twitched and brought her fingers and toes to life.

As she let out the deep breath she had involuntarily been holding in, Victoria became aware of the sharp pain that suddenly ached up her right arm and the right side of her lower back. Her head felt heavy and sore like she had cracked it on the concrete.

Suddenly, as her vision swam back into focus, Victoria realized that the Visitor that had taken her had been attacked by one of the roaming Mindless and that the Visitor had released its hold on her to defend itself. She had fallen backward onto the concrete before her body had 'regained' itself, and had cracked her skull on the sidewalk, as well as scraped the skin down her arm and back.

Victoria continued to blink, and becoming suddenly and acutely aware of her surroundings, she raised her neck and craned to find the Visitor and the Mindless, both deadly foes for her while she was hurt and defenceless. She saw a bloody mess that had previously been the Mindless attacker, lying in a heap on the concrete. Blood lay everywhere from its detached torso, and she could clearly see its severed spinal cord through her now sharpened awareness. The Mindless lay torn from the Visitor's strength and weight, and the giant form of the Visitor lay silent next to it.

Fear suddenly filled Victoria as she looked over the blood and debris from this battle. She couldn't understand why, but a fearful ache raged in the pit of her stomach like she had eaten a dead weight. She had to get away, and fast.

Victoria stiffly pulled her upper torso to a seated position and looked around for some cover. She saw an overturned SUV and a large army vehicle lying on the road near her that she vaguely recognized from a previous scouting mission. This was near the apartment building, but on the other side, heading away from the shopping mall she and Max had raided earlier and closer to the lake that ran behind it. The Visitor had certainly been taking her to its ship, but it had gone the long way around as it had no sense of the fastest route to take in this new environment.

Victoria tried to move her legs and found they were stiff and sore and barely able to move. She put both her hands on the ground and used all the strength she could muster in her weak state to pull her incapacitated legs along the concrete towards the closest cover of the abandoned vehicles. As she shuffled over the glass and debris that littered the road, she tried to concentrate on exercising the nerves and muscles in her toes and feet to get them working again. She was scared, not only of her violent and unpredictable surroundings but of having somehow damaged her legs and not being able to run from the impending danger that she knew lurked around every corner.

As she shuffled and twitched, her feet began to gain the light tingling sensation of having fallen asleep. She guessed it was a side effect from the Visitor's spell it had put on her. She looked over at the mass of Visitor lying in the middle of the road and realized there were several huge bloody gashes on its shoulder where the Mindless had tried to bite and rip into it. They were bleeding a mottled gray and purple that shined in the daylight.

Suddenly, the Visitor's shoulder began to twitch and spasm. The dead weight in Victoria's stomach dropped another inch or so, leadening in terror. She had seen this type of spasm before when the Mindless were transformed.

Victoria grunted in anticipation as she quickened her shuffling to the SUV. When she reached it, she forced her tingling and tired legs inside the broken window and wedged them under the seat that was now upturned against the sky.

The Visitor continued to spasm and thrash furiously. She knew the transformation took no more than a minute, and that this was a transformation she did not want to witness. Victoria placed her hands under the front seat and lifted her tired body into the sky and against the roof of the car, hidden from view of the Visitor over the seats of the SUV.

The Visitor suddenly sprang to life and thrashed its body around until it was in the standing position. It made a dark, grunting howl of noise as its beady nostrils sniffed the air. From her position in the SUV, Victoria could see the dark red-rimmed irises that were commonplace in the eyes of those that had been changed into one of the Mindless.

The Visitor turned and sniffed again, and with a sudden gasp, Victoria realized what it had found. It was the unconscious body of Ian, lying ten feet away next to the lifeless limb of the Visitor, both of which had been discarded when the Visitor had been attacked by the Mindless. Ian looked a bit battered, with bruises forming all over his face and body, but Victoria could see the slow rise and fall of his chest rose, responding to his beating heart.

He was alive, but not for long.

There was nothing she could do about it this time. A Mindless was one thing, and a Visitor was another, but a Mindless Visitor was something unimaginable that her mind couldn't even comprehend, let alone fight against it and win.

The Visitor sprang at Ian and began to tear him apart in the middle. Blood and entrails spurted everywhere as the Visitor dipped its elongated cranium towards Ian's body to soak its dark hole of a mouth in his blood.

Tears fell from Victoria's eyes as she watched her friend be eaten alive, helpless and immobile from inside an upturned

SUV. Her salty tears fell onto the hood of the SUV silently, but the Visitor lifted its bloody head from Ian's body, suddenly acutely aware that it was not alone.

The Visitor sniffed the air and turned its head towards the SUV. She felt her stomach drop as she realized that it had found her again, and this time one of the Mindless wouldn't step in to save her unexpectedly.

Suddenly a blinding flash of blue electricity snaked out from behind the upturned SUV and found its way directly through the Visitor's cranium. It zapped the Visitor; electricity stunned it for a second before the head fell apart in a sticky implosion. Green brain-like matter and purple–grey blood oozed from the Visitor's strong ropey neck where the head used to be, as the body slumped forwards, motionless and dead.

Victoria craned her neck and struggled to look after her, through the broken windowpanes of the SUV's rear windows and straight into the dark unblinking eyes of another Visitor. It had its long metallic gun pointed directly at the Mindless Visitor and upon its destruction, the Visitor tapped one of its suction-cupped fingers to a small button on the metal cuff on its wrist. The long gun suddenly folded up into itself to fit inside a small compartment that was in the underbelly of the cuff.

The Visitor that had destroyed its Mindless counterpart crawled over to the dead bodies and sprang around in an agile manner, kicking soft flesh here and there to ensure the complete destruction of all around it. It sniffed its beady black nostrils at the monstrous sight that was what was left of Ian, and satisfied with the result of his death, crawled closer to the dead limb of the Visitor that Victoria had severed in the apartment. The Visitor picked up the limb with its suction-cupped fingers and in a flurry of movement, released the metallic cuff from the arm.

The Visitor then threw the arm back to the ground, and still holding the metallic cuff, turned its back on the whole grisly scene and continued back in the direction of its ship.

Victoria could hardly breathe, and continued to hold her breath for as long as she could. She stayed wedged between seats, upside down in the battered SUV for as long as her body would hold her, too scared of her surroundings to make a move. She looked over at the army vehicle and saw a few half-eaten dead bodies in army camouflage uniforms lying around it, with marks of suicide plain to see in their skulls. She turned from the debris of an apparent Mindless feeding frenzy and let her mind adjust to what she had just witnessed, felt and experienced.

Finally, through the hazy fog that was clogging her brain and causing her eyes to droop in exhaustion, Victoria realized what she needed to do.

*****

Max was beside himself as he loaded up his weapons and prepared to go after the love of his life. Jacinta ran in front of him and tried to stop him, but he wouldn't have a bar of it.

"What exactly are you going to do?" Jacinta demanded of him. "You don't know what these things are or what they want. Are you going to just waltz up to their ship and ask 'Hey, can I have my wife back please?' and expect they are just going to give her to you? You're no good to us dead!"

"I'm no good to anyone without Victoria," Max bit back at her with determination in his eyes. Mia, Hulio, Diana and the children all looked on at the exchange in the hall with fear in their eyes. Frankly, at this moment, Max just didn't care.

"I don't believe that! Look at all you have done for us! Everything you both have done! Victoria risked her life to try and save a member of the group, and now you're going to give all of that up?" Jacinta sought to reason.

"I would give everything up for her," Max spat out.

"She's probably already dead Max," Jacinta proclaimed.

"Don't. Say. That. To. Me." Max barked through gritted teeth, toe-to-toe with Jacinta.

"Guys!!!" Jay yelled from the balcony of the common area where he stood staking out the new development that had taken place in the cross-street. "It's her! I see her! It's Victoria!"

"What?" Max could barely breathe as he turned from Jacinta and ran past her to join Jay on the balcony. Jay was right—it was Victoria! She was slowly making her way towards the apartment on the street below. Max could hardly believe it. He whipped his head around to stare at the others in disbelief, only to discover that Jacinta was gone.

"Oh no!" Max proclaimed and took off to the fire stairs after her.

Jacinta was already outside and pointing a heavy duty rifle directly at Victoria when Max burst out onto the street from their sealed exit. His heart leaped in his throat, thinking that he was about to lose the love of his life again.

Victoria was moving towards them, stunned and shuffling, exactly like the Mindless walked when they weren't on the hunt. She had the purple blood of the Visitor in a long messy streak down her pink t-shirt, and Max could see that her right arm and shoulder were covered in massive, bleeding scratches. She looked messy and tired and slow.

"Stay right there! Don't you come any closer!" Jacinta bellowed at Victoria, pointing her rifle straight at her head. Victoria continued to shuffle along in a haze, unable to grasp what was going on around her, before she suddenly stopped. Her vision was swimming and dancing in front of her eyes, and she vaguely comprehended that Jacinta was seeing her as a current threat to their group of survivors, but her friend's foggy brain couldn't formulate the thought that Victoria wasn't a threat.

"Jacinta, drop your damn weapon!" Max screamed at her.

Jacinta glanced sideways at him.

"I won't Max. You say you won't protect the well-being of the group, but I will. Someone has to make the tough decisions."

"She's not one of them Jacinta! Look at her!" Max pointed desperately at Victoria. He realized that Jacinta held all the power with the gun in her hands, but he wasn't prepared to risk Victoria's life again.

"She was taken by one of the Visitors Max. They could have implanted her with a homing device, a bomb … anything! They could have sent her back to kill us all!" Jacinta's voice sounded reasonable, plausible. They didn't know anything about these Visitors and for all, they knew it could be true.

"Look at her! She's not one of them! Please, let her go!" Max's voice filled with the desperation he felt. "Please! I love her!"

Victoria's head swam with blinding colours and flashing dark hues. She was about to faint. She could vaguely hear Max and knew that whenever he was around, she was in safe hands.

"Max …" she groggily whispered, and Max felt his heart break. His wife needed him, and this goddamn woman wouldn't get out of the way.

"I'm going to her Jacinta. If you don't let her come here, I am going to her." Max held up his hands to prove that there were no weapons in them, and he stepped slowly towards his wife.

"You're risking everything, Max! Everything!" Jacinta yelled at him.

"She could be fine! You don't know! You're right, she could be a trap sent by the Visitors, but she could also be fine. We need to talk to her and see what she knows and what she has seen. There is no point blowing her away right now. We need to be sure." Max stepped closer and closer to his wife, who had begun to sway in place. It didn't make her case any more convincing.

CHAPTER 4

Victoria was in quarantine for a little over thirty-six hours. They put her in one of the downstairs apartments in the building opposite the one that everyone was staying in. They all had a direct view into the apartment from their balconies in case anything went wrong.

Jacinta and Max cleared the bottom floor of Mindless tenants that had been roaming the hallways and made a blockade for her before Jacinta demanded that Max return to their own apartment building. He wanted to stay with his wife, and tried to convince her, but Jacinta was firmly rooted in the belief that even if there were something wrong with her—something planted by the Visitors—he would lie and say there wasn't so that he could bring her back into the fold.

Instead, Jacinta swapped shifts with Jay and Danny in watching over Victoria, after insisting she inspect her for tracking or homing devices. Once cleared, Victoria lay unconscious for a vast majority of the quarantine before finally waking up and tending to her scrapes and wounds. She tried to talk to the group and tell them what was going on, but Jacinta had made it very clear that she was not to be listened to.

Finally, after another medical examination, Jacinta decreed she was safe to return to the fold. Max was overjoyed and met her downstairs where Victoria fell into his arms and cried as she held on to him.

"Don't ever do that to me again!" Max protested. Victoria sobbed into his arms, fitting perfectly into the space of his chest.

"I'm sorry! I'm sorry!" Victoria wept, turning her head to look up at him. They kissed passionately, uncaring of those around them. They walked upstairs and Victoria re-joined the group in the corridor leading to the common area. She felt like a lifetime had passed since she and Max were returning from their raid on the shopping mall just days before.

The whole group joined them in the little kitchen in the main area, where Victoria stood in front of them like an army soldier with Max by her side.

"What happened out there Victoria?" asked Diana in her thick accent. Victoria addressed the whole group, "What happened is I found out that the Visitors can be stopped," she said.

"How?" demanded Jacinta, still on edge.

"When I was being pulled back to their … ship, I guess it would be called … I was in a fog," Victoria launched into her story. "Like everything was too bright, and I couldn't control my body. I went with the Visitor because that was all I could do—everything it was forcing me to do. I remember vaguely seeing one of the Mindless attack the Visitor, and I could feel its pain inside—like it was attacking me personally. All of a sudden my vision came flooding back as they fought and I was able to hide in an upturned car.   From that position, I could see that the Visitor quickly killed the Mindless, but was bitten badly and turned into one of them."

"Are you serious? It was a Mindless? How is that even possible?" Jacinta exclaimed. Jay started freaking out, eyes widening.

"I thought I was done for" continued Victoria. "But then I saw another Visitor come and kill the Mind-less Visitor. It killed it with the cuff that was held on its wrist— you know, the cuff that was attached to the arm it was trying to save when it attacked us. The cuff turned into a gun and when aimed at the monster's head, and it imploded on itself." Victoria exhaled and waited for her group to take this information in. She didn't think it was possible, but Jay's eyes widened even more.

"What happened to Ian? Where is he?" Mia asked quietly.

"He's gone," Victoria paused, thinking back on the horror she had witnessed, "I'm sorry, but there was nothing I could do for him."

"He knew about them. He knew about everything; about how it all started. He didn't tell us a single thing. Why didn't he say?" Mia asked the group.

"He wouldn't have told us. If you had a hand at the end of the world, would you have announced to the group of people you're surviving with?" Jay asked.

"Whatever he knew and whatever he did, he led them right to us. They probably targeted us because they knew he was here!" Jacinta exclaimed, angry with their deceased friend.

"I don't think he did it on purpose Jacinta," Max defended, "I don't believe he knew that these Visitors were going to come back for him."

"Well I guess we will never have a chance to find out, will we?" Jacinta continued. "What is really going on here Max? We don't know anything and the only man who might have known kept it to his bloody self—and even worse, led them straight to us!"

"I think they would have come regardless of him being here or not, Jacinta," Victoria answered, "And even if we don't know why they're here, there is something I do know. I think I can use the gun they wore on their wrists. I think I know which button it pressed on the cuff to dislodge the weapon," Victoria announced the kicker to her news.

"Do you think it would work on a Visitor that hasn't been affected by the disease?" asked Max, leaning forward on the island in the middle of the kitchen.

"I'm not sure. I think it would work on both the Mindless and Mindless Visitors. It killed the Visitor when it had been infected, as well as all the Mindless that attacked the ship that landed earlier," Victoria answered.

"Is it worth the risk?" Jacinta demanded.

Everyone looked around at each other. They looked at the life that they had created huddled on the top floor of this apartment block, forever risking their lives to get food, water, and supplies. They were killing and shooting the Mindless every day and never easing that feeling of always searching for the safe or secure. Now with the Visitors in the picture, they were more unsafe than ever.

"I think it is," Victoria answered for them all. "I understand if you don't want to do it, but I believe that this is no way for us to be living. We can't just hide in here and hope for it all to go away. The Visitors are here now and however they were aware of the current situation, I don't think they're going to leave. They'll find us eventually and who knows what will become of us then? We know this area better than them, so wouldn't it be better to have the element of surprise?"

"Well you already know that I'm in," said Max, looking lovingly at his wife.

"I'm in too," piped up Jay.

"Me three," Danny said, "I think there is a good chance this could work."

"I can't live like this anymore," said Mia with sadness in her heart. "I have no one from my family left, I want to avenge their deaths, and I'm willing to die trying."

Hearing a fourteen-year-old girl agree to die for the cause made Victoria almost well up with tears. She had hoped one day she and Max could have started their own family, but they had never had a chance, living the life they did. Maybe they could, if this plan worked.

Hulio nodded in agreement as well, which caused Diana to whimper and start speaking to him in her native language. They had a hurried, heated conversation in their own world while the group looked on. From her mannerisms and heavy movements, Diana did not like what Hulio was saying and finally ended the conversation in a disgruntled "harrumph."

Hulio turned back to the rest of the group and spoke to them in broken English, "I will fight. But Diana, Alejandra and Jose need to stay behind."

"We can't protect them if this fails," Victoria told him, making sure her message was obvious.

"Diana is strong. She will fight for them," Hulio announced slowly, and everyone nodded, looking at Diana sadly. She hadn't done many supply runs and hadn't faced much since they all holed up in the apartment, choosing to tend to her motherly role and making sure the floor was clean, and the food was cooked. If this failed, chances were unlikely that they would survive.

"This is ridicules!" Jacinta shouted. "You are all just willing to go to your deaths over this?"

"So what do you think we should do Jacinta?" asked Max, turning angrily to her.

"We could go, leave this area and find somewhere new to survive!" Jacinta declared like it was the most obvious thing in the world.

"Is this really surviving? Is it really living?" Max asked, "What if there is no one else in the world? You really want to just live with them? What if there are other Visitors? As a group with a well-formed plan we can handle it together, but not alone.

You're a strong fighter Jacinta. We need you," Max finished sadly.

"And you'll leave Diana and Alejandra and Jose to their deaths?" Jacinta cried angrily, not caring about Diana and Hulio's faces that were twisted in fear and pain at her.

"Alejandra and Jose cannot fight. It's smart to leave them behind with their mother," Max told her.

"And because Mia's motherless you make her fight?" Jacinta declared. Mia's startlingly bright blue eyes flashed with anger at her.

"I make my own choice to fight," Mia told them. "If they can, they need to go on. They still have so much to live for, and have been less involved in so much horror." She paused, still wounded by Jacinta's declaration. "I would fight even if my own mother was still alive. It's the right thing to do."

"I won't be a part of this. You may not value your life, but I do. I didn't go through what I have been through, and I have not done what I have done to throw it all away now on some plan that we don't even know will work." Jacinta angrily declared, shaking her head. "I won't do this with you."

Victoria had suddenly had enough of her protests. "Stay with Diana, Alejandra, and Jose then!" she cried, "Cower in the corner and call it protection. We all know the truth behind it— you're a coward!"

"I don't have to stay and listen to this!" Jacinta roared.

"Then don't," finished Max.

Jacinta glared back and forth between Victoria and Max. They were always the ringleaders and always the saviours. She had had enough of it and didn't want any part of their foolhardy plan. They didn't know her or what she had been through, and they certainly didn't need to. She shouldn't have to prove her right for survival; she had done that enough just by still being alive.

"Fine," Jacinta said, finally quiet. She turned on her heel and walked out of the main area to her single apartment where she slammed the door shut.

The group watched her go silently and mourned the loss of Jacinta's support. Finally, Victoria turned back to her companions who were staring at her and Max with wide eyes.

"Ok, here's the plan …" she started..

CHAPTER 5

The next morning Victoria, Max, Hulio, Jay, Danny and Mia crowded around the doorway to the stairwell on the first floor. They were dressed in their survival gear: jeans, cargo pants, and heavy jackets; weapons stored into pockets, sheaths, gun pouches and boots. Victoria skimmed her newly-greased manual chainsaw blade and drew blood on her thumb. She smiled at her favourite weapon and swung the chainsaw into the pouch on her back.

"Everyone ready to go?" Max asked, clicking the safety on, finally stowing his pistol into his gun belt. The members of the group nodded in unison.

They were ready.

Standing at the door, the group could hear a low moan from the inside stairwell, stifled by all of the concrete constructed for the apartment building's fire safety.

Jay opened the door to the downward stairwell and held up his own pistol while the rest of the group crouched low and prepared themselves for action.

They had cleared the opening levels of the stairwell when they had first set up in the apartment building, and the amount of Mindless that they had initially found in there was astronomical. They had started out innocently as human beings trying to escape the breakout and had ended up sealing themselves into an unforeseen but horrifying fate in the small concrete space.

The group had stowed all of the workable vehicles they had rescued on their previous scouting missions in the bottom car park of the apartment building. However, an outbreak had occurred within the complex when Ian had failed to shut the garage door in time after Victoria, Max and Jacinta had returned from a supply run. They had encountered a lot of the Mindless on that particular early run to the nearby fruit and vegetable markets and had narrowly escaped. Unfortunately, they brought the horde back with them and after a bloody attack in the car park, the foursome made it to the stairwell and through the door to the first floor. Locking them in, it left countless Mindless creatures in the cement stairwell, leaving the group with no way to access the cars they had scavenged.

The only way to get to the cars was to force the Mindless out down the stairwell and into the parking garage, where there were light and space to fight successfully. Peering in now, the stairwell was pitch black. There had been no electricity for years, and the darkness was both ominous and overwhelming. The group, led by Jay, walked quietly down the stairs, trying to keep their footsteps as soundless as possible.

A groan began to emanate from the next landing down; Jay pulled a long knife out of his sheath and broke forward from the crowd. He approached the Mindless quietly and drove the knife straight into its head through an eye. He had gotten good at a quiet assassin-style approach thanks to all his years playing violent video games from the couch.

Despite the quiet kill, the Mindless grunted loudly and fell to the ground. The stairwell was quiet for a moment before more groans loudly started. The dying grunt of the Mindless had alerted others in the stairs.

With no time to waste, the group burst forward to meet the horde head on, running down the stairs. The closest in the group stopped, gouging the Mindless in the stairwell with their various weapons and continued on their way as if they had just stepped around a puddle on a rainy day. There weren't many of the Mindless on the actual stairs, they were spread out on the staircases and landing, but they were each taken down with precision and expertise.

It was strange the things you could get used to—and become good at.

Running down the stairs after killing them all, the group burst through the door and into the basement car park. It was lit dimly with sunlight from small rectangular windows near the roof. The Mindless were wandering aimlessly around the garage, among the leftover vehicles full of looted possessions.

With the sound of their abrupt entrance, the Mindless turned as one and saw the group bunched together at the stairwell door; warm, moving and alive. Seeing the group on offer was like calling for a takeaway pizza back when such things existed. Victoria grabbed Max's arm, just as the stairwell door snapped securely shut behind them.

For a moment in time they were all frozen; counting down to another bloody encounter.

They didn't have long to wait.

The Mindless horde began to move towards them, picking up pace from a slow amble to a savage run in no time

"Spread out!" yelled Victoria as the Mindless began their attack. She grabbed Max's hand and ran across the car park into a small storage cage that was no bigger than a toilet cubicle and right in the middle of the vast garage. She barely glimpsed Jay and Danny heading off into one of the storage cages that lined the edge of the wall of the parking garage, and Mia and Hulio being swiped at by a nearby Mindless as they ran to secure their own separate storage cages.

Reaching the cage, Victoria ripped the door open and threw herself in, kicking a few small decomposing boxes out of the way. Max followed suit and slammed the cage door behind them. He pulled a screwdriver from one of the pockets in his cargo pants and shoved it quickly into the cage wall and the door, securing it from being opened, just as a large group of Mindless slammed into the cage at a full sprint; the metal recoiled in response.

Victoria and Max stepped back from the walls of the cage, but even side-by-side in the middle of the small space, the Mindless were still able to shove their dead rotting arms through the cage and reach out for them, clutching at shirts, jackets and for thin air. Victoria felt a tug on her hair, and she turned, seeing that a wall of the Mindless had appeared at the cage wall behind them as well.

Getting this close to them, what startled Victoria wasn't how much their gnashing teeth and rotten skin looked the same as the next; it was how different they all looked when together. She could practically see the human being that was beneath this devastation on each and every single one of them.

There was a young woman with dirt-streaked blonde hair and a professional-looking, tailor-made suit now marked with blood and torn in various places. An African man with a large gouge in his forehead, but his large brown eyes, which once would have shone with hope and possibility, now were a muddy gray colour with red-rimmed irises and glowed with unquenched bloodlust. There was an attractive looking Cajun man with mahogany-coloured hair, who had died with a neatly trimmed goatee, some wrinkles between his eyebrows, and a smile that would have lit up Las Vegas if only it weren't gaping at her for her blood.

Still, despite the fact that each of the Mindless had different features, were different sizes, different heights and had once held different pieces of humanity within them, they were for all purposes, all the same now with their vacant looks and brilliant red irises, rotting skin and gaping wounds, reaching into their cage to devour Victoria and Max.

Victoria shook herself out of her stupor, which had only lasted a few seconds at best. She pulled a knife from a sheath stuffed into her boot and drove the blade right through the muddy, red-rimmed eyes of the African male. He made a long sound that was halfway between a gasp and a growl and slid to the floor, driving the blade out of his skull with a wet pop as he did so. Next to her, facing the other way, Max was using the same killing technique with a wooden stake he had fashioned from a broken baseball bat, found on a scouting mission and taken as a weapon.

Victoria moved on to the Cajun and drove the blade through his eye socket, just as his strong scrawny hands reached through the cage towards her. He too slid down to the floor, the cage wire cutting deep into the flesh of his arm before it followed the rest of the body out and down to its final resting place on the cement.

Victoria and Max moved from Mindless to Mindless, cutting them down and leaving them piled on the floor outside the cage. Congealed, almost purple blood and entrails splattered all over the concrete, with bits of rotted flesh stuck and hanging on the wire of the cage that protected them. One after the other, the Mindless tripped over their predecessors to get to Victoria and Max, and one after the other they were slain with cold efficiency. When Victoria had disposed of the last struggling Mindless, she turned towards Max, who wiped the sweat from his brow with the back of his hand and breathed a sigh of relief.

They looked over at the other cages to see if the rest of the group were alright. They could see mutilated, rotting bodies piled around the cage in which Jay and Danny had hidden, but five Mindless were trying to reach through the pile of dead to the cage where Mia and Hulio had sought refuge. They couldn't reach the brains of the Mindless to do any permanent damage and were stuck in the cage.

Max pulled the screwdriver from the cage door and gripped it. He pushed the cage door open with a struggle, the door wedging on a pile of torsos and decaying limbs. Victoria bent down to the concrete floor and slid her arm through the gap at the bottom. She grabbed a severed arm and threw it across the floor. A Mindless, trying to get through to Mia, turned slowly towards them as it heard the wet slap of flesh on cement.

Throwing the arm from the door paved the way for the cage to open further and Max was able to slip through the gap. On seeing this, the watching Mindless started running towards Max so he ran straight to it, meeting the monster and driving the screwdriver through its eye socket. The strike stopped the Mindless in its tracks, sending it to the floor with a wet growling gasp.

Max started towards Mia and Hulio's cage, stepping over the now still Mindless mess. He pulled out his pistol and pumped one round into the back of each of the heads of those Mindless still crowding the cage. They dropped instantly, and the group was enveloped in an overwhelming silence.

They had killed them all.

By this time, Victoria had pushed her way out of the cage and ran over to Max. Together they grabbed a variety of arms, flesh and ragged rotted bodies and shifted them from the cage door. Mia and Hulio pushed their way out and sighed in relief that no blood was lost—at least on the side of the living.

Jay and Danny pushed their way out of their own cage and joined the group in the center of the car park, breathing heavily and feeling the adrenaline coursing through their veins.

"You guys know the drill," Victoria told the group, and they nodded in agreement. They knew what they were getting themselves into. Mia and Hulio turned on their heels and walked towards an SUV still parked in a spot, picking the lock and throwing their canvas bags onto the back seat.

Jay and Danny nodded at Victoria and Max once more and packed their rifles into a flatbed truck parked near the entrance of the car park. Victoria and Max looked around for their own set of wheels and spotted a shiny black motorbike lying in a corner parking space. They looked it over, determining that besides a few scratches, it was in good shape.

"Can we keep it?" Victoria asked cheekily, turning to Max with a sly look on her face. He grinned at her, grabbed the bike by the handlebars and swung his right leg over the seat. As he bent down to hotwire the bike, Victoria took off in the opposite direction to open the garage door.

Victoria pulled the chain and started to raise the heavy metal door that acted as a shielded gate to the parking garage. It used to be automatic, but with the electricity turned off there was no choice but to do things by hand. Once the garage door reached the top, she pulled the chain sideways and secured it to the side of the door to keep it open, then hopped onto the back of the motorbike which Max had successfully hot-wired. Max revved the engine and a thundering rumble echoed through the concrete garage, as Victoria gripped Max by the waist and rested her chin on his shoulder.

"I love you, Victoria," he said, with only a hint of sadness, knowing that it could be the last time he was able to tell her that.

"I love you too Max," Victoria answered, all too aware. It was their ritual to say so before the start of every scouting mission, and this time was no different.

The bike purred in response as Max accelerated out of the driveway, followed closely by the flatbed truck and the SUV. The bike and the SUV turned left and started the drive, while the flatbed turned right.

The battle had begun.

CHAPTER 6

The flatbed had the longest way to go and Jay Welles, and Danny Masters had been entrusted with using their speed and knowledge of the area to get them around the Visitors without raising suspicion. They were headed to the mall, which was within walking distance of the apartment block, but with the Visitor's ship having landed straight in the middle of the area, they had to drive the flatbed out and around the lake to enter the mall from the south side.

Jay had lived in the area with Danny before the outbreak of the Mindless had begun. He had actually lived in the apartment block the group all currently resided in, but on the second floor. He and Danny used to have minimum wage night jobs and had mainly spent their days smoking weed, eating junk food and playing an obscene amount of video games. Their love of warfare games had come in handy when the invasion began. Jay missed those days, missed the games, but he hadn't had a puff of a joint in years, and that was what he missed the most in this terrible world.

Jay and Danny had been aware of the attacks around the world, and had heard tales of murder, cannibalism, and riots in the streets, but it had always been someone else's problem. These sort of stories had been headlining the news even before the dawn of the outbreak, so it was hard to pinpoint when it had officially begun—and that's what made the news so irrelevant to him. The violence kept coming, but the world just kept turning.

He had been at the very same shopping mall on the day of the local outbreak. On reflection, it was all so straightforward and easy then. He had been at an electronics store, checking out new DVD's he wanted to download and get high to later that night. Finally deciding on one, he put them down just as the occasional screams had started. He looked towards the store entrance and saw a few people sprinting past the doors. They were the fitter ones who were more alert—two skinny blonde girls in athletic clothing and a tall man in a business suit with long legs.

This was strange, and with a furrowed brow, Jay had slowly walked to the entrance to see what was happening, thinking that someone had just been robbed. He was weirdly drawn to these kinds of incidences—like staring too long at a car crash on the side of the road when you drive by—and he was keen to make the most of the situation. However, when he reached the entrance, he was forced to jump back as the rest of the crowd came running past the store's entrance, screaming and gasping for air. They were people from all walks of life: mall cleaners in uniform; mothers clutching on to baby bundles, pressed to their shoulders with their strollers long forgotten; there were quite a few thirtysomething professionals with their whole lives ahead of them; and there were teenagers with backpacks and skateboards, skipping school for the day.

One casually dressed man had flung himself into the electronics store, knocking past Jay and taking off towards the back room, yelling at shoppers to flee.

Unexpectedly scared, Jay looked in the direction that the group had been running from and could hear screams and wet slapping sounds pierce the suddenly stale air of the mall. He looked over at a nearby shop, two doors down in the direction people were running away from. Through the stampede of people, he saw a redheaded woman had fallen down. She was gasping in pain and had her arms outstretched, trying to pry herself away from a skinny Asian man in ripped clothing who was bent over her. Jay was horrified to witness the seemingly weak man claw into her back, then lean down and take a raw and bleeding bite out of the woman's shoulder.

Shocked, Jay's eyes widened, and he looked around through the quiet fleeing crowd. He saw many others like the man, bleeding and catching shoppers as a lion would take down an antelope. It was exactly what he had seen in all these games and movies, and he didn't feel the least bit heroic.

He felt terrified.

Jay looked around for a hasty exit and saw the crush of the crowd stampeding over each other at the staircase. A few unfortunate people were pushed over the edge of the railing as they tried to crowd around and run down the stairs, only to fall with a sickening thud on the tiles of the bottom level.

There was no way he would make it out alive following the crowd, and he was damned sure he wasn't prepared to risk going into the crazy, violent throng in the middle of their vicious attack.

Jay saw a large department store opposite him and glimpsed an opening at the back wall of the store that was unmistakably a service exit. He knew it would be his only way out.

The crowd started to thin out at the entrance to the electronics store, and Jay took the chance to run towards the opening of the department store across the hall. As he sprinted directly across the cold tiled walkway, he looked to his right and got a much better look a large number of the rioters ravaging the mall and attacking shoppers … and incredibly, shoplifters taking advantage of the situation. Severed arms were thrown, faces were torn in mid-scream, and blood splattered across the walkway. In his shocked state, Jay slowed slightly to take in the sight, and a few of the Mindless noticed his desperate sprint. They dropped the pieces of living flesh that they had been gorging on, and rising from their kneeling positions, were intent on having Jay as their next meal.

Jay sped up and ran straight through the department store towards the service exit, aware of the Mindless following him picking up speed. He knew the only way to escape was to try and lose them so he ran ragged along aisles flinging baskets, pillows, knives, forks—anything, behind him trying to create some obstacles between himself and the Mindless. He succeeded in slowing them down with the distractions, but he had to jump out of the way of others that were circulating the department store aisles in search of their own victims. Jay reached the very back wall of the store and pushed the service exit swinging doors open.

A bemused ethnic man in dirty canvas overalls looked at him and started shouting, saying he wasn't allowed in the back room. As Jay pushed past him, the man cried out in shock as the Mindless that had been following Jay went straight for him.

Not warning this man was one of Jay's biggest regrets, and he carried it with him to this day, and probably would forever.

Jay had continued with his exhausting sprint, pushing open the back door of the service entry and finding himself at the cold and forbidding back loading dock of the mall. It smelled strongly of metal, and the air was colder and drier out there.

Without pausing, Jay jumped off the loading dock ledge where trucks usually backed up to, and without pausing, took off towards the street. He could hear the desperate screams of the ethnic man as he was steadily devoured, and behind that the screams and cries of others trapped in the mall; but all Jay could do was run, back to his home and relative safety.

*****

Jay and Danny now stood at the back dock of the mall where Jay had made his escape before running to the apartment to warn Danny. They had just rolled the flatbed up to the dock and opened the doors with caution and arms at the ready.

It was silent as the grave, and just as foreboding.

Jay and Danny carefully put one step in front of the other, silently stalking up the ramp next to the back dock. They pointed their silenced pistols and darted their sharp eyes, looking for any sign of danger.

Finding nothing, the pair continued their slow walk to the service door that led to the back of the department store. Jay took a deep breath, remembering how he had left things.

The door swung open with a creak that was deafening in the silence. It opened to the back staffing area that seemed even more cold and unkempt, a bleak cement block. The three Mindless that had pursued Jay were drifting uneasily in the sectioned off room, and he finally got a good look at the humanity of them. The small but vicious group was made up of a bulky bald-headed brute of a man in an oversized ripped trench coat covered in blood; a small Asian woman with congealed blood now dried on her chin; and a black-haired bespectacled woman in a store uniform.

They turned as one towards Jay and Danny at the sound of the creaking door. As if the cord had been pulled on a lawnmower to crank it up, the group started growling and gnashing their teeth, making ready to run at the boys as their adrenaline kicked in.

Before they had a chance, Jay and Danny levelled their weapons and shot silenced bullets straight into their heads. They weren't ready to cause a scene just yet.

Once the Mindless had died for a final time, Jay and Danny stood in the silence before becoming aware of soft shuffling movements on the cement floor. Jay walked over to the middle of the circle of now still Mindless and was horrified by the source of the noise.

The ethnic man he had pushed past during his escape was lying face down in the middle of the floor. He was struggling to lean up. He was clawing on the cement, but to no avail. He was missing both his legs and one of his arms, which Jay could see had been thrown aside, partly eaten. His torso and left arm had large purple bite marks all over them, and thick, congealed blood covered the entire surface of the floor area he was lying on.

There was practically nothing left of this man, and he had been subjected to a painful death and horrific rebirth because of Jay.

Jay kneeled down next to the man, just out of reach of his weak and bony fingers. His eyes started to well up with tears.

"I'm sorry," Jay whispered to the man. "I'm sorry you didn't even get a chance to make it out. I could have grabbed you and brought you with me, but I didn't and for that I'm sorry. I hope what I'm about to do will make it up to you."

With that, Jay pulled a knife from his sheath and drove it straight into the back of the man's now soft and rotten skull, destroying what was left of the brain that had now been turned into a Mindless mess. With a wet gasp, the man's head thudded to the floor, and they were left with silence once again.

Jay got up off his knees and returned his knife to its sheath. He turned and looked at Danny, who was looking at him with sombre eyes.

"It's this way," Jay pointed and showed Danny out of the door.

The department store was dark, and it was easy to hear the soft grumblings and moaning of the Mindless within it. Because of the large aisles circulating every area of the store, Jay and Danny were able to follow the corridors and sneak past lost and wandering Mindless, who ran the store now.   They walked slowly and carefully, trying to avoid the thrown furniture and homeware supplies that scattered the floor. Danny picked up a small bathroom mirror and used it to see around the corners that marked the ends of the aisles to ensure their safe passage.

They walked the excruciatingly long aisles to reach the front of the store and hid behind the closest shelf of aisles near the sensor detectors at the entrance. Danny used his mirror to make sure there were no Mindless in the surrounding area, and while he was looking, Jay gazed over at the open department store that he had been in when the outbreak began.

His eyes found several lifeless bodies lying in the store among the clutter of electronic equipment; one of them being the man that had run past him when the world had still seemed reasonable. Jay had to shake his head to erase the thoughts and memories of that day and focus on their mission at hand.

"OK … Go!" Danny whispered, and the two crouched down and shuffled quickly out of the store, avoiding being seen at all costs.

Outside in the corridors of the mall, Jay had time to take in the carnage. Objects once desired and considered 'must haves,' now utterly unnecessary junk, lay everywhere, and pools of blood and ripped flesh stained the once gleaming white tiled floor. Light streamed in from the building's sunroofs as he and Danny moved quickly and quietly down the corridor to the staircase where Jay had seen many people fall to their deaths. Their bodies lined the grand entrance and Jay couldn't help looking at these people he had seen alive not so long ago. It was all so surreal.

Danny elbowed Jay out of his haze, and he looked up to see a Mindless swaying silently and unseeing on the staircase they were about to climb.

The pair neared the start of the staircase and looked at the blood-smeared glass of the elevator that was encased by the stairs. Some unfortunate people had died horribly trying to escape in the elevator, and their mangled bodies and possessions were littered around the small area. A Mindless with long straggly blonde hair and a face full of dark dried blood stood in the middle of the bodies, trapped with nowhere to go.

It saw them as they approached the staircase and started banging its head on the glass wall of the elevator; its eyes wide and its mouth hungrily gaping at them. It couldn't get past the dead bodies that surrounded it to even get close, so Jay and Danny slowly climbed the staircase with it watching them with gnashing teeth as they ascended.

They passed a litter of debris on the stairs. There were a few heels and handbags lying on the steps, and even a sneaker that still had a foot inside it severed at the ankle. Reaching the midpoint of the circular staircase, the Mindless that had been swaying, turned to take them so Jay lodged his knife into its bloody eye socket, which had the eyeball ripped out of it. With a groan and a squelching sound, the Mindless sank to its final resting place on the stairs.

Jay and Danny reached the top and looked around this new floor. A few Mindless stood in wait next to two half-closed stores, but their backs were to the pair so Jay and Danny were able to sneak by undetected. These Mindless drones could be used for the later battle.

The two men walked silently on the blood-stained tiled floor. They were heading into the thick of the Mindless plague within the mall—the food court. Many people had been sitting there during the first outbreak, and many of them hadn't left. Sneaking up behind a juice bar counter at the perimeter of the food court, Jay looked out into the penned-in area and saw hundreds of Mindless. They were bruised, bloody and decaying; swaying silently, shuffling in the enclosed space.

Jay and Danny dropped on bended knees behind the counter and looked around behind them. Danny pointed at a fire exit that was a few stores from the juice bar, and Jay nodded solemnly. He turned to his best friend, who had been through the entire outbreak with him, and gave him an awkward man hug. He then got to his feet, still crouched down low, and took off quickly towards the fire exit.

Jay pushed open the door and looked down the cold, cement corridor. He listened intently and didn't hear any groaning from the fire exit. He turned back towards Danny and stuck his right thumb in the air.

Danny nodded solemnly and took a deep breath. In one swift movement, he stood up and jumped onto the front counter of the juice bar. He let out the loudest yell he could muster and aimed his gun in the air. Danny fired his bullets into the tiled ceiling and was met with hundreds of gray unseeing eyes with red irises, turning in his direction.

The snarls and the growls started almost immediately as the deafening smattering of bullets died away. The Mindless all started towards him, adrenaline pulsing and the pace getting faster. The closest of the Mindless ran straight into the juice bar with their arms spread open to encase him, but Danny deftly hopped off the bench and headed in Jay's direction and the fire exit door.

Jay had propped the door open with a box that had failed to be delivered on the day of the outbreak, and he waved Danny down through the corridor. He got a look out into the food court and was confronted with the sight of hundreds of decayed bodies sprinting towards them.

Jay and Danny ran as fast as they could. Behind them, the Mindless came after them with astonishing speed, reaching out with their bony decayed fingers and filling the corridor with their animalistic groans.

CHAPTER 7

Riding in the passenger seat of the SUV with Hulio Flores, Mia Cavallari looked out the window, lost in her thoughts. She was as haunted and silent as the graveyard of empty streets outside. It could all end for her today if she didn't fight back against the Visitors that threatened their precarious survival; but among a horde of Mindless, it hadn't really been surviving anyway.

Mia had been at school the day of the outbreak, and it surprised her now how extraordinarily ordinary the last day of civilization had been. She remembered grumbling over having to take a math test and gossiping with her best friend Beth Deloraine when she heard that the class heartthrob Daniel Ryder had taken a shine to her. Mia remembered going up to Daniel that day in the school halls and having him laugh in her face when she suggested going out sometime. He called her names like 'loser' and 'virgin,' while the popular girls Kay Stevenson and Natalie Hyde looked on and laughed.

They had always been tormenting her. Mia wasn't a popular girl and in hindsight, she had probably had the most ordinary of school experiences—the kind of experience that almost everybody had. The kids seemed to find their own clique and do their own form of backstabbing until they were forced into the real world and got the hell out of school. The real world knew that the popular jocks would later be running errands for the nerds, and the popular girls would be pregnant at seventeen, claiming benefits well into their lonely future.

Looking back, Mia found it so unfortunate that she had spent so much time studying for her maths exams and writing essays for English. She had hoped that she would eventually move on to be a journalist and thought she would have to spend the majority of her time with her nose in a book. If she had known her classmates Kay, Natalie and Daniel would never get the chance to be anything more than they were then, maybe she would have acted differently. She would have regarded it less like the world was swallowing her whole with high school embarrassment, and more like the world was available to consider her every whim and desire—after all, the clock had been ticking. They just weren't aware that it would end so soon.

Thinking back to the experiences she missed out on, Mia would have had that first drink offered to her at a party she and Beth had crashed that New Year's Eve at Beth's older cousin's house. She would have had the nerve to tell Kay what she thought of her when she stuck gum in her hair during English.

She would have begged Beth to get on the bus with her the day it all happened.

After Daniel had laughed at her and pushed her books from her arms, he had strolled off down the hall with Kay in tow, looking forward to a good make-out session behind the trees at the perimeter of the school. Beth helped Mia pick up her books and apologized profusely for making her a laughing stock.

"I'm so sorry Mia!" Beth cried, pushing her blonde flyaway ponytail out of her face, "I heard from Nicky that Daniel was sweet on you and was fixin' on asking you out but was too scared."

"Beth you know Nicky is in Natalie's pocket! How could you believe a single word she says?" Mia had asked, fighting back the tears in her blue eyes.

"I don't know! I'm sorry! I thought I was helping!" Beth was exasperated now. She was always a sweet-natured person who only saw the best in people, which caused her to act first and reason later. Mia was aware that Beth had honestly only wanted to help her friend, but at that moment Mia was so embarrassed that she had to get out of that school.

"I have to go, Beth," Mia said decisively, pushing past her to walk out the front doors that were in the opposite direction to where Daniel and Kay had headed.

"I'll come with you! We'll hang out and talk about what Kay would look like bald! It'll be fun." Beth tried to follow her, and bless her heart, tried to make the pain she had caused better.

"No thanks, Beth. I need to be alone." Mia shut down the conversation and spun on her heel to walk out the front doors and get on the school bus waiting out the front.

Mia forever regretted the last words she had said to her best friend. If she had just forgiven her for being an unwitting part in the stupid prank, Beth would have gone with her to the farmhouse that day, and she would have survived. At least survived a bit longer.

Mia's memory jolted back to the day the farmhouse was overrun with the Mindless and the way they bit into her father's shoulders and tore her mother's arms from her body as she tried to run for the back door. Maybe it had been for the best that Beth hadn't returned with her. Maybe Beth would have met the same grizzly end that she could have met at the school. Mia didn't know what the best situation was anymore.

Back on the day of the outbreak, Mia had jumped onto the bus like her life depended on it—and it had, but at the time she had been thinking about her social life and not her actual life. She barely greeted Herb, the fattened old bus driver who had always been so cordial to her. Mia sat in her usual seat halfway up the bus and slid over to the window, putting her face on the cold glass to help the redness of embarrassment in her cheeks subside.

Mia looked through the window at the other students milling around and saw Beth emerge from the school front doors looking sad and lonely. She saw a group of kids in beanies and camouflage gear spark their cigarettes out the front, also sparking anger in Mrs. Gould, the uptight librarian.

The bus Mia was on was quite empty save a few other kids she didn't really look at. Kay and her friends loved to call it the "corn fed bus" because it took the kids on the outskirts of town to and from the school. It was mostly boys and girls, like Mia, from the local farms, they were not in with the cool kids.

Mia's father, George Cavallari, had been a veterinarian and bought the farm to help nurse sick horses and livestock back to health. They lived on the outskirts of town among a few stockyards and a winery. Mia had loved living out there with her family. Her mother June Cavallari was reminiscent of the classic 1950's housewife, and Mia had been the youngest of three girls; her older sister being a headstrong brunette named Georgia with the city in her sights. Georgia had moved out of home early in life because she didn't feel she fitted into the old-fashioned country lifestyle Mia's father and mother had created for them. However, Georgia had certainly come running back when the Mindless had taken over and turned the boyfriend that she had lived with into one of them. Mia had been glad when Georgia came home. She had always looked up to her for getting out of the country and was happy to know that she had survived the first outbreak in town. It was Georgia's nature to survive.

Mia's second eldest sister Joan had gotten married young to a dim-witted but kind-hearted man named August Burns. They had two children by the names of Rosie and Oscar and lived on the farm with Mia and her parents. It had been torture growing up in a house that had two babies running around in it. Mia had always felt left behind by her sisters and left out by her parents and her extended family, because all of the attention seemed to fall on Rosie and Oscar and how they were being raised. She felt invisible at school and just as invisible at home.

Mia sat looking out of the window of the bus as the city sped by. They had to pass through the main hub of the city and a park before they reached the road that led out to where Mia lived. Because most of the kids on the bus lived out of town, there were no stops in the main area of the city.

Mia first thought something was wrong when the bus trundled by a convenience store on the main city street. The glass windows at the front were decorated with a red jelly looking stain of a handprint, and she could see into the store that there was quite a hive of activity at the back of it. She couldn't make out what it was and figured perhaps maybe some of Daniel's older friends were being juvenile and pranking the place like college kids who would use toilet paper to tee-pee a house.

Herb, the bus driver, started coughing loudly from his front seat, and it pulled Mia out of her trance. She looked at the rest of the people on the bus, and nobody seemed to be paying the convenience store the least bit of attention. The kids were laughing and hitting each other excitedly, glad that the school day was done, and they could go home and meet the twilight hour between the oppression of school and the rules of their home life with video games and possibly a swim in the nearby creek.

Mia turned her head back towards the window and saw a few people looking a bit tattered and wandering aimlessly down the street. She saw one of them catch a glimpse of a woman in business attire on a cell phone and start to quicken their pace to reach her. When they started running the woman stopped in her tracks and turned around, pulling the cell phone from her ear and looking like she was in total shock.

The bus flew by the scene quickly, and Mia was unable to see what happened to the long lost friends who had just found each other on the street. She had had no reason to believe anything sinister was going on.

However, as the bus continued its ride down the main street, Mia was caught off guard by a large group of people who were running in all directions. She would have thought that by the amount of individuals who were running that there was some kind of marathon on, except they were all in normal clothes like jeans and skirts and even high heels instead of the usual sweatpants and sweatshirts.

The bus stopped at a traffic light near the park and Mia saw the group of people catch up to them. Suddenly hands were banging on the windows of the bus next to her and all around her. Terrified faces were screaming at her, and kids inside the bus were yelling as well. Mia had no idea what was happening as the group tried to get onto the bus with them.

A woman used her high heel shoe to smash open the window behind her and Mia ducked down to avoid the impact of the glass. She could hear Herb yelling at the front of the bus, but she couldn't be sure of what he was saying. All she could be sure of was that underneath all the screaming and the yelling, Mia could hear some slippery wet growling noises getting louder and louder.

Mia crept back up from her crouching position and looked out the window, past the bloody streaked handprint that was now right next to her face on the windowpane of the bus. All around her was a flurry of movement, and she realized that people were fighting amongst themselves.

Blood splattered everywhere as people drove their sharp fingers and teeth into the soft flesh of others. The only way Mia could describe it was like several bears attacking a herd of deer. People screamed while others growled and bit into their flesh easily like a knife cutting through warm butter.   They were strong and super-fast. Others were still trying to get onto the bus, and the victims were trying to gouge at the attackers with shards of glass from the broken windows of the bus or from anything they could get their hands on. An old woman was among it all trying to hit her attacker with her handbag and another man in a smart business jacket with matching trousers was brandishing his closed umbrella at a stranger.

Many people fell, motionless and unseeing as their attackers dove on top of them and started biting into their flesh, pulling their organs out of their bodies. Mia had never seen so much blood, and of course had never ever seen body parts ripped from their resting places.

The attackers ripped into intestines, arm sockets, and chests; blood and organs spilling from their mouths, over the fronts of their shirts and pants, up to their elbows. There was nothing left of a few people before the mutilated bodies that were still whole enough started to twitch and pull themselves up from the concrete, turning to the bus and the other cars on the street looking crazed and savage.

It had all happened within a matter of minutes. Mia joined in with the screams that pierced the inside wall of the bus and Herb put his foot on the accelerator, speeding forward through a red light and hitting a car out of the way to continue on his frantic drive. Mia hit her head against the window because of the impact of colliding with the car and rubbed her rapidly swelling temple as the bus careered on.

Herb sped all the way out of town, and Mia couldn't erase the bloody visions swimming in front of her eyes. Kids in the bus seats next to her were screaming and crying in terror, and she was among them, sobbing silently in horror. Herb slowed the bus and stopped outside the scrapyard where he regularly did and got up from his seat, something Mia had never seen him do in his overweight condition.

"Kids, Get out! Go home! Tell your parents what happened if they don't already know and bar your windows and doors. Get somewhere safe and stay there. Go on! Get!" He yelled at the kids. They were all frozen in terror in their seats.

Herb pressed the palm of his hand to his horn and blasted it, which shocked the kids out of their stupor. Grabbing their belongings, they scrambled out of their seats and out of the bus doors in a hurry, with Mia among them.

Kids took off in all directions to their homes and Mia ran with them up the road. It was silent up here except for the soft twittering of the birds that normally comforted her after a hard day at school. Today she could only hear the blood pumping through her veins, her heavy puffing as she ran and the sound of her sneakers hitting the gravelled road.

Mia ran up the gravel track that led to her farmhouse and both cursed and thanked God for it being situated on the outskirts of town. She ran screaming into her house and wouldn't stop until her father emerged from his study, wiping his glasses on the edge of his buttoned-up shirt.

"What in the world is going on?" her mother asked, coming out from the kitchen and wiping her hands on the apron she wore over her yellow dress. She caught sight of Mia with her swollen temple, messed up hair and tear-streaked face. "Goodness! What's happened to you?" Mia's mother asked.

Mia's father bent down on one knee and looked her in the eye. She could barely talk from trembling as she began to blurt out everything that she had seen and everything that had just happened.

*****

Mia could hardly believe that she was back in that same town and going back to the same high school that she had been in on the day that the Mindless had taken over. Hulio drove to her high school as quietly as possible, and they backed quietly up to the closed school gate.

Mindless were everywhere, and Mia realized that her classmates had not even been able to leave the school that day before the horde had attacked. She had gotten out just in time, or she would have been one of them.

Mia saw the cigarette smokers ambling listlessly around the school's front compound, as well as some of the best-dressed and attractive Mindless she had ever seen, with straight blonde hair, jeans, and tank tops—and gaping bloody mouths. She saw Mrs. Gould with her tight bun now falling out around her face and blood all over her usually crisp white blouse.

And she saw Beth.

Beth was standing, swaying slightly, by the entrance of the school and covered in blood from head to toe. Her blonde hair was still in the ponytail she had flicked out of her face as Mia ran away from her and the blue eyes that Mia had made smile so many times were dull and ringed with the red irises; common among the Mindless.

There was no other way out in the plan that Mia and Hulio had devised. Mia had to use Beth to pull the other Mindless out with her. Right then and there, Mia resolved to put Beth to rest, if it was the last thing she did.

The school gate kept the Mindless in, but even so, Mia and Hulio crept from the car as quietly as possible and made their way to the trees lining around the school. They walked silently through the trees with their guns drawn as they circled around the school to get to the back entrance. There were less Mindless at the back, and more of a chance to collect the ambling souls.

Mia and Hulio climbed a tree with low hanging branches and hoisted themselves up and over the metal fence of the school. Mia landed in a crouched position, pulling a knife from her belt and looked around to take in the familiar landscape of her old school.

Mia nodded at Hulio, who landed with a soft thud next to her, and they took off across the open playing field at the back of the school. A few solitary Mindless were scattered amid the overgrowing green grass but Mia cut them down efficiently and silently with the knife before they had a chance to run at them. They reached the edge of the school building and slowed down, coming to a stop at the gray brick of the back of the structure.

Mia reached out with her hand and felt the rough and cold material that had housed so many of her childhood memories. Today was the day for making new ones.

Mia peeked out past the corner of the brick wall and saw a group of Mindless milling around the back entrance, unable to get into the school because the doors were closed. She smiled cruelly when she recognized the blonde hair of Kay, the short jean skirt that had been a signature look of Natalie's, and the letterman jacket that Daniel had been wearing.

Kay's naturally tanned skin was now pale and decomposing. She had a large, congealed bite on her forearm, but she was otherwise not mauled. Natalie's jean skirt had been ripped and was even shorter than it usually was, she wasn't wearing shoes, and her legs were covered in blood. Daniel was worse off. He had blood splattered clothing and bits of flesh hanging off his chin.

Mia rounded the corner, keeping as close to the brick wall as possible. She walked quietly down the stairs with her knife drawn and sharp, gleaming in the sunlight. Natalie was the first Mindless to be alerted to her presence and turn towards her. Her now muddy brown eyes flashed as the red of her irises caught the sunlight. Her eyes narrowed, and she started growling at Mia from deep within her throat.

Mia ran forward and thrust her knife straight through one of Natalie's once pretty brown eyes. Natalie made a harsh gagging sound as Mia withdrew her knife and Natalie crumpled into a heap onto the ground. Mia wiped the congealed blood on her jeans and turned towards Kay and Daniel who had now also been alerted to her arrival.

Daniel took a head start and Mia turned and ran back up the stairs. They followed with lightning speed, and Mia gave a yell as she rounded the corner of the school. Hulio let Daniel past him and jumped out as Kay followed close behind, taking her down.

Mia turned and shouted obscenities at Daniel as he ran closer and closer to her. He barrelled on top of her, and she fell to the ground, using her newly strong arm muscles to hold him up as his teeth and arms gnashed for her. She slowly moved her right hand to hold him directly square in the middle of his neck, and she could feel the pressure of his teeth and strong jaws as they tried to take a bite out of her.   She pulled her left hand backwards—the one that was holding the knife—and drove the blade straight up through the weak flesh of Daniel's stomach. She felt the knife lodge and dragged it upwards through his decomposing body and towards his head, lodging it in his chest between his ribcage.

Daniel's red irises pounded in his skull, and he let out a growling shriek as congealing purple blood splattered out of the knife wound and out of his mouth, falling onto Mia's face as she tried to turn away from the spray. This immediate gasping pause allowed Mia the chance to put her whole weight behind her, rolling him over so that she was on top of him instead.

Without a moment's hesitation, Mia pulled the knife out of his ripped body and drove it directly through the forehead of Daniel's soft decaying skull. She saw the red in his irises fade as he relaxed backward onto the concrete, motionless, cracking the back of his soft skull.

"That's for turning me down asshole," Mia spat at him before she pulled herself off him. She turned towards Hulio, who was standing above a slain Kay. He took in the purple blood that covered her from chin to hips.

"I'm fine. Not a scratch. Let's keep going," Mia told him, and Hulio nodded with understanding. She wiped her forehead with the back of her hand and took off after Hulio down the concrete stairs and into the school's main hall.

Chapter 8

Max and Victoria Stone had turned the bike off and stowed it quietly next to the front doors of the local gym. There weren't many of the Mindless out the front of the large lime green painted building, but they could see them wandering around on the inside. Dark red handprints and smudges covered the front glass sliding doors of the gym that had stopped working when the power had been cut.

Max thought back to the day of the outbreak; he had been at this exact gym after work. He had a depressing office job, selling medical insurance to customers over the phone who would later call up and abuse him when the company refused to cover certain operations or procedures. It was not his fault—the company had been set up to cut corners and keep costs down and unfortunately it meant that he had to take the brunt of the client's anger.

It was a far cry from where he wanted to be. He had aspirations to become a doctor but was stuck studying part-time just to make ends meet.

Day in and day out, he and Victoria had worked demoralizing office jobs to pay for a modest lifestyle. They saved up what money they could to cover the ever-rising costs of living, but it didn't give him the opportunity and the freedom to pursue his real love of helping people. In the days before the outbreak, he got up each morning and put on one of his neat shirts with a tie that felt like a hangman's noose tied around his neck.

Thinking about where the world had ended up, Max saw his past life selling medical insurance as a disaster. If he had known what was to become of the world, he wouldn't have bothered studying, or he would have pushed himself harder to meet his goals sooner. Hell, maybe he would have taken out a bank loan and gone around the world with Victoria. Maybe they would have been lapping up the sun on an island in Costa Rica when the outbreak began. They could have been visiting the giant heads on Easter Island or even taking a roller coaster ride in freaking Disneyland.

But no, he had been at the goddamn gym, just like he did every day of his monotonous life.

Still, Max had always enjoyed working out. He kept fit, and it raised his self-esteem, arming him with endorphins to face the next boring day at work. Now every day was a workout just to survive, and he was ultimately thankful for the high intensive activity that he had done daily back then. It had helped keep him agile and ahead of the Mindless during their attacks. After all, the unhealthy people of the world had been the first to go since they were unable to outrun the Mindless.

Victoria usually joined Max at the gym, but on the day of the outbreak she had had to work late so Max went alone. He changed into his track pants and sweatshirt and ran on the treadmill as he normally would. The gymnasium had two floors. The cardio and weights area was a large, echoed metal void with high ceilings and cold temperatures. The upstairs area was a lot warmer and had more muscle-building machines with long windows looking out over the stadium area.

A small group class was working out next to the cardio area on a series of jungle gym equipment, like bags and ropes and weights. He had never joined in one of the classes, but Max often saw the people in the small group classes running up and down and doing jumping jacks out of the corner of his eye during his own workout.

Half an hour in and the class was still going as Max went upstairs to finish off his workout with some crunches. He took notice of the people in the upstairs room as they pumped iron with their headphones in and music devices switched on and loud. They were all in their own world, concentrating on their workout and not on the other people around them.

Max finished his last round of crunches and got up to do his stretches in a small room to the side. As he pulled his ankle up behind him to stretch he glimpsed of a flurry of movement in the mirror. He dropped his ankle to the ground and turned around to face the area where the movement had come from; it was coming from the stadium below.

Max walked slowly over to the large window, pulling his headphones out of his ears, shoved them into the pockets of his track pants and peered down at the people in the gym. He saw the small group class running from one side of the gym to the other, and he breathed a sigh of relief he hadn't realized he had been holding in. They were just finishing off the cardio in their class.

But when the people didn't return on their run, and frantically started climbing on gym equipment, Max looked closer. He saw a very overweight man dressed in black workout gear lying on the ground and an African man in a crisp business shirt and dress pants performing CPR on him. The class instructor, dressed in a matching black woollen tracksuit, was kneeling next to him.

Max felt sorry for the overweight man and silently hoped he was ok. Clearly, he had overdone his workout. It was only when Max saw a pool of red start to flood out beneath where he lay that he looked a bit closer.

The instructor and the well-dressed man were bent over the large man, tearing through his shirt and into his stomach. They were pulling his insides out with superhuman strength, slinging blood everywhere, and stuffing the slimy, messy entrails into their dripping mouths.

Aghast, Max's eyes widened, it was hard to take it in as he scanned back to look at the faces of the people in the class. A woman with a brunette ponytail and a pink tank top let out a huge scream, and the instructor turned and looked at her, a piece of liver falling out of his mouth. The instructor rose to his feet and picked up speed, running straight for her, pushing her down on the treadmill she had climbed on, ripping into her as she continued to scream.

The well-dressed man also rose to his feet, alerted by the screams of the class, and started hurrying towards the other people who tried to fight him off, but to no avail. Max was stunned with horror as blood and insides stained the treadmills, the rowing machines and the lime-coloured brick walls of the lower stadium area.

As the bloody commotion raged on, Max turned his focus to the overweight man. His eyes had opened, and he was writhing on the floor in a spasmodic motion. He jerkily got to his feet and as he stood, a pile of his intestines, meat and blood fell to the ground at his feet.

"Impossible!" thought Max, but sure enough the fat man with a large gaping hole through his black shirt started towards two scantily clad female bodybuilders in a far corner. They were in their own world, backs turned, music turned up, with their attention on their muscles.

Suddenly the fire alarm sounded, and the red flashing lights and matching noise pulled Max out of his stunned stupor. He heard a series of screams, slightly closer to him, and he looked towards the door.

Athletes and people who had been working out downstairs were now running up the stairs and bursting through the doors that led to the area where he was. Max saw three of the Mindless creatures trying to make their way up the staircase. Their various injuries made the stair climb difficult, but their eyes sparkled with lust and determination, and they rose up the stairs as fast as their bodies would allow.

Max realized that the only exit out of the gym was straight through the room that held all the equipment and past the doors that were now barred openly by these crazed humans. He watched one descend on a poor older man in a white singlet who had been working out on a bench press, unable to get away in time.

Just next to this man, who was now writhing in pain as the Mindless bit into his neck from behind, was a large row of dumbbells ready for lifting. Max knew it was the answer.
Without any time to lose, Max took off at a sprint towards the dumbbells, glad that his muscles were warmed up and ready to go after his workout. He cleared the short space in a few large bounds and grabbed one of the heaviest dumbbells he could swing.

The Mindless who had been chomping into the man in the white singlet saw Max's run and immediately dropped the man, who cried out in pain as he hit the floor, trying to stem the blood that was flowing from the gaping wound in his neck. The Mindless moved closer to Max, and he saw only one option. Max lifted the dumbbell and smashed one of the weighted ends straight into the face of the Mindless. With a thick grunting sound, the Mindless fell sideways with the force of the hit and landed with a dull thud on the ground. The man it had just bitten startled backward against the wall and whimpered at the sight, as the blood continued to flow from his wound.

The Mindless made another grunting sound from its resting place on its back, its red irises glaring directly into Max's piercing blue ones. Max saw that its jaw had broken completely and was hanging on to its mangled human face by a few fragments of bone and flesh. Teeth had been shattered loose, and the chin had become concave.

As the Mindless made a few more grunting sounds and attempted to get up, Max knew it was going to attack him again until one of them was dead. Without hesitation, he shoved the weighted dumbbell into the head of the Mindless with all his strength. With a crunching and splattering sound, Max closed his eyes to avoid the blood spray as he repeatedly beat into the Mindless human's skull.

When the movement beneath him stopped, Max peeked out of one half closed eye at the motionless and completely unrecognizable mess that was a human being only moments ago. Max felt all his breath leave his body—he had never been hunting before, never hit an animal with his car and had never killed anything, not even a pet goldfish. It was like a huge weight was suddenly shackled to him, and he could barely breathe from its intensity. He had killed someone.

Suddenly Max became aware of the sound of rapid breathing next to him. He tore his eyes away from the wet flesh at his feet to look directly at the man in the white singlet. His arms had dropped from grasping the bite wound at his neck, and his eyes were now ringed with an angry red around the iris. He twitched profusely as he snarled and growled at Max, diving towards him. Max used his well-honed leg muscles to spring backward, and the man in the now blood-stained white singlet got caught around the dead body Max had been kneeling over.

Jumping back, Max bumped straight into the arms of another Mindless, and he could feel its hot breath on his neck as it went in to take a bite. Determined to make it home to Victoria, Max swung the dumbbell he was still holding up to the side of his head and quickly ducked out the way so that the weight caught the Mindless creature behind him square in the face. He felt as well as heard the thudded squelching sound as the dumbbell pounded into the head of the Mindless, knocking it back to the window, which broke with a shattering sound, causing the Mindless to fall backward through the window and onto the floor of the stadium below, spraying everywhere around it with blood.

Max looked through the window and saw that the fight had caused quite a few red-rimmed eyes to turn in his direction with interest.

He pulled his gaze from the angry eyes below and stepped backward to avoid the reach of the man in the white singlet who was trying to get up over the dead body of its fallen comrade. Max turned his back on it and started towards the exit, right through the thick of the outbreak.

He passed a woman in workout gear sitting on one of the machines, screaming as one of the Mindless tore at her left wrist and another one ripped into her right thigh. Max continued running and used all of his strength to lay the dumbbell into the side of the head of the gym instructor, who had just come up the stairs and was eyeing the fast moving Max as its next meal. The instructor went down on impact as the dumbbell crushed the side of its skull and Max had to close his eyes and mouth momentarily as blood and brain matter splattered out.

Max continued running and dropped the dumbbell to the floor as he approached the office desk at the gym entrance. He glanced over the counter as the poor blonde receptionist behind it was being eaten alive by three Mindless dressed in gym clothes. Max barrelled around the corner and jumped down the flight of stairs four at a time. As he rounded the banister, he saw that he was being pursued by two of the Mindless—a man and a woman in sweatpants with blood dripping from bite wounds on their arms and legs.

Max put on speed and jumped down the last flight of stairs, taking off towards the glass entrance doors to the gym. As he left, he hit a large red exit button that closed and sealed the entrance doors in the case of a fire and reached in his pockets for his car keys.

Life as he knew it had changed in minutes.

All he had to do was get home now and pray that Victoria was there waiting for him …

*****

"Come on Max, they're waiting for us," Victoria told him, pulling Max back into the present. She stood outside the gym doors with a long-barrelled pistol and a large hunting knife in hand. Max nodded to shake off his recollections and walked forward to join his wife.

Victoria picked up a large rock and threw it through the window of an office that was situated just off the main entrance. She cleared away the broken glass, and they both climbed into the office that was scattered with paperwork. Victoria walked over to the closed door and listened for a moment, but they could hear no growling or grumbling sounds from the Mindless outside the room.

Victoria slowly turned the handle on the door until they heard a faint clicking sound. She pulled the door open, and they looked out into the hall. The coast was clear.

Max led the way, his own semi-automatic gun at the ready. Together they crept into the main entrance like a pair of professionals; Max leading the way and Victoria a few steps behind. Their pace was slow and steady, with knees bent in preparation for a sudden burst of energy, movement, and adrenaline.

With none of the Mindless wandering the main entrance area, Max and Victoria were able to stalk up the stairway unmolested. They reached the gym's reception, and Max spotted the same blonde receptionist lying behind the desk. She was rotted and mangled, with her skin decomposing and her insides splayed all around her. Dark blood stained the carpet she was lying on, and she had tiny insects buzzing around and writhing inside of her dead body. Max silently wished he could have said something, wished he could have saved her, but it had been too late.

Victoria stepped behind the desk and pointed her pistol at the ready, searching for any signs of movement. When she found nothing, she re-joined her husband, and they walked forward into the central hub of destruction.

Thankfully, most of the Mindless had regathered in the downstairs gym area, where the first signs of the outbreak had occurred and where there had been more people working out. Max noted through the windows that there were a few of the Mindless in the upstairs stretching area where he had been when it had first begun. He pointed silently for Victoria, who nodded and brandished her pistol in the direction of the downstairs area. They needed a big crowd.

Victoria and Max crept as quietly as they could to the main doors of the downstairs area. Max looked out at the crowd who wandered aimlessly among blood splattered exercise equipment and recognized the fat man with his intestines still hanging out, the brunette in the pink workout gear who now had no arms, and even the man in the business shirt with a bloody hole in his eye socket. Max couldn't shake the feeling that he was facing his ghosts, and in many ways, he guessed he was.

Victoria nodded at Max, and they stood up together. Max shifted his gun off safety and let it rip, spraying the tin roof of the gymnasium with a smattering of bullets that echoed like thunder throughout the stadium. He felt the kick with each round that exited his gun, and he watched dust and debris fall from the heavens.

The Mindless in the stadium turned in every direction, caught off balance by the echo that the gunfire was making. They started snarling and growling, with their red-rimmed irises flashing.

"Hey!" Victoria let out a loud yell to alert the Mindless to their position. Max felt shivers go down his spine as the gun stopped spraying bullets and a hundred blank and staring eyes turned in their direction.

It all happened so suddenly. The Mindless took off for them, running to the stairs and feeding on adrenaline as they all crushed together to try and get up the staircase. Victoria and Max pulled back and turned to leave, only to face the man in the white singlet who had been in the stretching room.

Without a moment of hesitation, Max fired a shot straight into the man's face and peppered his body with bullets as the gun continued on its semi-automatic range. The man growled and gasped as he fell to the floor and Max thumbed off the automatic clip.

By now, the fastest of the Mindless had reached the top of the stairs so Victoria and Max took off towards the entrance that they had just come through, pausing momentarily at the staircase to ensure the Mindless were still following.

Max jumped down the stairs as he did before, with Victoria picking her feet up as she took two at a time and concentrated on not tripping. A Mindless woman with a decaying face barrelled down the stairs next to them and landed on the middle flight of stairs, ending up prostrate on the landing. She gasped and reached for Victoria, who kicked her square in the face with her steel capped boots.

Reaching the main hall, Victoria and Max ran into the office they had first entered and jumped through the broken window. The Mindless ran after them; reaching, falling through and crawling to catch up. It was a stampede, without order and with one bloodthirsty purpose.

Max saw the slowest of the Mindless crowd the main entrance hall and press up against the glass doors. Their teeth were gnashing in hunger, and a few at the front were even being squished against the glass. Their faces were smearing decay and rotten congealed blood over the glass and windows. The glass began to crack like a spider web under the pressure.

Max jumped on the front of the bike, revving the engine while Victoria picked up a rock, identical to the one they used to break in, and lobbed it with all her strength through the glass windows of the front door. The glass shattered into a thousand little pieces, and the Mindless at the head of the mob suddenly fell through the raining glass and landed on the front stoop of the gym.

Victoria turned backward, ran and jumped onto the back of the bike with Max, just as the lead fallen Mindless were being stepped on by the ones at the back in their desperation to reach the fleeing pair.

The air was filled with groans, rumblings and the wet sound of sticky decaying bodies being trampled underfoot in the stampede. Max thrust the accelerator, hurtling the bike forward as they headed in the direction of the Visitor's ship.

"They're gaining on us, keep going!" Victoria shouted in his ear over the loud roar of the motorcycle as they gunned it up the abandoned streets with a horde of Mindless behind them.

CHAPTER 9

Jacinta Reinhart stood looking out over the balcony of her bedroom on the sixth floor of the apartment block, muttering to herself. She felt guilty as she watched the group drive away towards their destinations, but felt a flash of anger as Victoria and Max roared out of the apartment's car park on a big black motorcycle.

Always showing off those two; saving the world and saving the group. Being the big heroes of the day and being so in love. It was nauseating. Even in an apocalyptic world, Jacinta couldn't get away from the 'it' couple.

Jacinta had been in love once—just once. He was a tall, well built dark-skinned man with a shaven head and a row of tattoos that he covered up with his crisp white business shirt and expensive slacks. His name was Don Romero, and he had been the big bad boss in the financial planning agency where she had worked before the whole world had been ripped apart at the seams.

Jacinta had hated her job as a receptionist until Don Romero walked through the door. In fact, she had hated just about everything. She had gone to college and studied accounting because her father had told her to, but she hadn't amounted to anything since she had graduated, beyond getting people coffee and answering phones. She had wanted to be a kickboxer when she was younger after she watched her father train boxers and fighters in his urban street gym. Her father had done some permanent damage in the ring so he forced her into a "safe" job to avoid her following in his footsteps and making the same irreversible mistakes.

Jacinta felt like her whole life had been a mistake. She had exactly one friend in the financial planning agency—a Caucasian woman with curly brown hair who was forever forcing Jacinta to join her and her skinny boyfriend for after-work drinks. They were always trying to set her up with one hopeless guy or another and Jacinta smiled and went along with it because she had nothing else to go home to besides an empty apartment and a boxed frozen meal.

She had known they were getting a new CEO for a while and had thought very little about it until she walked into the boardroom and was greeted by his dazzling smile. He was so sweet and tough and attractive that he caught Jacinta off guard.

So she started popping the top buttons on her crisp white blouses and crossing her legs in a provocative manner whenever he walked by. When he had hardly noticed her, she 'accidentally' slipped laxatives into the coffee of the chipper gay man who acted as the CEO's assistant, causing him to have several sick days off, forcing Jacinta to cover his duties. It was all she needed to get the attention that she desired.

The day of the outbreak may have been the happiest day of Jacinta's life. She had been openly flirting with Don during the days before the epidemic reached the office and she remembered being called to him mid-morning with his coffee and notebook. She sat down opposite him and began writing his daily memos, but he seemed out of sorts. That's when she noticed the bandage on his left hand.

"Are you OK Mr. Romero?" Jacinta had asked in her most seductive voice, indicating the bandage on his hand. "Can I get you the first aid kit?"

"Oh, this thing? It's fine. Some homeless man bit me ten minutes ago when I was outside the coffee stand getting my midmorning coffee with some of the investors. Can you believe it? Ridiculous!" Romero had told her. In her mind in the present, Jacinta could hear the alarm bells ringing, but at the time she had only wanted to play the part of the sexy nurse.

Jacinta summoned all of her courage and got up from her seat, placing her notebook on her seat behind her. She walked around his large oak desk, and he rotated in his chair to face her as she did so, a questioning look on his face. She pulled the hem of her pencil skirt up slightly and pushed her thighs on either side of his legs, sitting down on his lap.

"Oh poor boy," Jacinta whispered in his ear. "Let me take care of you." She started kissing his neck, and although he had been caught by surprise, his response was eager and impatient. They had begun kissing passionately, and he spun her around on his chair and laid her on his desk, clearing everything out of the way.

Pressed between his hard muscles and the hard oak desk, Jacinta was in heaven as he kissed her lips, her neck, her chest and back to her lips again. She breathed him in as he reached below and pushed her skirt to her waist, exposing her carefully chosen underwear. Her exploratory fingers reached between their bodies and handled the buckle of his belt, whipping it undone and moving on to the buttons on his pants.

Pushing the zipper down and springing him free, Jacinta felt her expensive underwear rip at the seams as his large hands clutched and pulled them out of the way. He was stronger than she expected, but she loved every minute of it. Don's kiss deepened and she felt him enter her. He was long and hard, and Jacinta let out a gasp as she felt the full weight of him inside her.

They stopped for a moment and breathed, taking in the sensation of each other like they had melted together. Don began to slowly push himself in and out of her, Jacinta responding rhythmically. His hands touched everywhere, pressing down her blouse and popping the buttons on her shirt as he freed her soft breasts from her lace bra.

Don's mouth followed suit as they continued their tour of Jacinta's body; she could barely do anything but let out soft moans of pleasure. Her bare bottom began to pound violently against the cool wooden desk she lay on, and she could barely keep herself together as she felt the sweet release coming.

Jacinta pulled slightly out of their rhythm to meet Don's mouth with a passionate kiss, and she felt his lips slacken a little like they had not quite met hers, but Jacinta was so happy she could barely notice this subtle change in passion.

Don, slowing slightly, pulled back from Jacinta and she felt him depart her body like her soul was being removed. He pulled her body off the desk with an undeniably strong force before quickly swivelling her around and bending her over the desk again. Jacinta's chest pressed against the wood and she watched her breathing make small patches of condensation against the tabletop. Don held her down in place and entered her again, causing another excited gasp of surprise and pleasure to escape Jacinta's lips.

As their rhythmic pounding continued with Jacinta's toes curling in ecstasy inside her high heels, and all she could see was the wooden desktop, and all she could feel was her own happiness and pleasure. She didn't realize that it was changing.

It was slow and subtle at first. Jacinta's heavy and ragged breathing slowly fell back into its normal rhythm as she felt him finish, but Don Romero's breathing kept exaggerating and soon turned into a deep growl in her ear. Jacinta was still looking down at the desk and noticed a small droplet line of thick blood splashed onto the wood.

Jacinta pushed herself up and turned back towards Don, who was leaning heavily on top of her. She looked into his chocolate brown eyes and was startled to suddenly find the irises were rimmed in a bright glimmering red. The blood droplet had slid out of his mouth, which was now turned into an otherworldly snarl.

As adrenaline pulsed into Don, he readied himself to spring at her and attack, and in an instant, Jacinta had pushed him backwards, right into the wall. She pulled her pencil skirt down and ran around the oak desk, bending her knees and regarding him carefully. She had no idea what was wrong.

"Don? Don … I'm so sorry if that's not what you had intended. I'm sorry if I caught you off guard, it's just … I've been noticing you around the office and …", Jacinta's rapid explanation turned into a squeal as Don ran at her, clearing his oak desk in one adrenaline-fuelled bound.

Jacinta crouched herself flat and used the kickboxing techniques that she had been trained in to kick Don squarely in the chest. He was flung backward against his desk, causing it to split and splinter wooden shards everywhere. One of her nude high heels stuck out of his chest; Don seemed not to even notice and simply righted clumsily to his feet, taking another lunge at her, gnashing his teeth and snarling.

In a quick movement, Jacinta kicked off her other heel and engaged Don with a few other boxing moves that she had picked up in her father's gym. He took each punch with ease, despite the surprising strength behind it. He grabbed her, and she spun her leg under him, toppling him to the floor. Don grabbed her leg, and Jacinta fell after him, straight on top of a sharp wooden shard from his desk that was sticking up from the ground.

Gasping from the pain near the bottom of her ribcage, Jacinta could feel the foreign object piercing her side. Yet despite the pain, she was distracted by the sudden shrieks of terror and rapid movement in the office behind the window shades she had closed when she first entered his office for their meeting.

Trying to climb forward to her feet, Don grabbed her ankle and made to bite her. Jacinta kicked back with all of her might and felt her bare foot collide evenly with Don's face. His grip didn't waver, though, so Jacinta turned to face the man she had developed strong feelings for as he tried to shove her ankle towards his gnashing mouth.

Thinking quickly, Jacinta grabbed the edge of the wooden shard that was the cause of the pain in her side and pulled with all her strength. She gasped in pain as the shard dislodged itself from her flesh, with blood quickly rising to the top of the wound.

She felt Don's body weight press once more on top of her as he grabbed her leg and moved his face closer. His teeth were gnashing; he was so close to taking a huge bite out of her calf.

With no time to think, Jacinta turned the shard around and drove it forward, straight into Don's face. The shard speared straight through one of his once beautiful chocolate brown eyes with a splattering of blood and matter. His snarling mouth let out a sudden choking sound and the blood drained from his face as he slumped in a heap. Don's grip on her leg eased, and he lay lifeless in a pool of his own blood and shards of his desk at her feet.

Terrified, and completely in shock, Jacinta pulled herself to her feet with her hands on her wound, trying to stem the flow of blood. She was trying to come to terms with the idea that Don viciously attacked her and tried to take a bite out of her—how could that be? It made no sense at all.

Jacinta gingerly let go of her wound and ripped the arm off the sleeve of her white shirt, which was now splattered with blood. She shuffled over to Don's now shattered oak desk and picked up a row of tape that had been flung to the floor.

She fastened a hasty bandage against the hole in her side before gingerly skirting around Don's dead body and heading towards the office door.

After all that had been happening to her, Jacinta had forgotten about the outer office sounds she had heard during Don's attack. She opened the door, expecting to meet police or the other concerned office workers, but she was greeted with pandemonium. Bloody bodies lay fallen on the floor or slumped over desks, high heels discarded and office supplies thrown everywhere. Some of Jacinta's co-workers were kneeling over the dead bodies and ripping into them like they were a big juicy steak. Blood and entrails were splattered everywhere on them as they turned to face Jacinta, sniffing the air as she limped out of the door.

Jacinta saw her friend with the curly hair leaning over the body of a man she vaguely recognized from the lunchroom. He was in a smart suit that was covered in blood and he was missing his nose and his left ear. Her friend had bitten them off and was in the process of chewing them up when she turned to face her. Her unremarkable hazel eyes were now rimmed red around the iris, just like Don's had been, and her blood-covered mouth let out a wet, choking roar.

Horrified, Jacinta didn't hesitate in taking off for the elevators in the main hall, but her usual speed was slower than normal due to her wound. Her curly-haired friend and a few others were gaining on her as she reached the silver tarnished doors of the elevator. A decapitated body lay across the gap in the door, wedging the elevator open. The controls were blurting out a series of annoying 'bings' to warn users of something stopping the doors from shutting.

Jacinta jumped over the lifeless and blood-covered body, which caused the elevator doors to fully open again. Once inside she turned and bent down close to the gaping bloody hole that was the neck, pushing it out into the hall by the shoulders. It took all her strength to do so, causing pain to rip up her wounded side, but just as she thrust him out into the hall, the elevator doors started closing. Through the gap, Jacinta watched in horror as her friend and the others reached the hall. The two others dove for the headless body and started trying to tear into him, but her friend reached out to Jacinta with her blood-covered fingers. With a menacing snarl, the elevator doors shut completely and started to take her to level one.

Jacinta backed against the wall of the elevator and started breathing raggedly, tears welling up in her eyes. The elevator music chimed merrily all the way through her descent from one horror into a world of horror outside.

*****

A loud explosion disrupted Jacinta's shocking memories. She jerked her head upwards and looked out over the balcony, seeing three large hordes of the Mindless closing in on the Visitor's ship in the middle of the intersection. Movement was everywhere as the Visitors were springing from their ship and putting an end to the Mindless that were clawing their way into anything alive within their reach.

Jacinta heard a loud scream that was too human to ignore. She looked down and saw three Visitors crawling around the midsection of the apartment building they were in. She had been too busy thinking about Don Romero to notice them approach on their routine search for human survivors.

Jacinta remembered with a jolt that she was supposed to be watching over Diana, Alejandra, and Jose while Hulio fought in the battle. She burst off the balcony and out of her apartment, sprinting down the long white corridor to the main area. Diana was huddled in a corner with Jose, but Alejandra was nowhere in sight. Diana started sputtering in rapid Spanish, pointing towards the far end of the corridor.

Knowing the answer to an unasked question, Jacinta took off back down the corridor she had just run down and took to the fire stairwell as fast as she could. The scream had sounded like it had come from the third floor, where they had set up all the bathrooms.

Leaping down the stairs three at a time, Jacinta felt like the run was taking way too much time. Reaching for her sidearm, Jacinta got to the third-floor landing and used an adrenaline-fuelled kick to break open the secure door to the stairwell.

"Alejandra!" Jacinta yelled, making her way along an identical corridor to the one on the sixth floor. Hands on her gun, she ran as quietly as she could, listening to any kind of sound to alert her to Alejandra's whereabouts.

Behind the fourth door, Jacinta saw a bright blue light illuminate the darkness of the corridor. She used all of her strength to kick the door in and went in gun first.

In the middle of the emptied lounge room, the small girl stood still and silent as a Visitor towered over her on its elongated legs. It had broken the window behind it when it had discovered Alejandra.

Jacinta wasted no time in firing off several rounds into the Visitor. It turned its steely gaze towards her and let out a shriek as the bullets dug into its gray flesh. Before her eyes, Jacinta watched as the Visitor's flesh began to heal itself over with a clear slime, before healing each bullet wound in its entirety.

In a fit of anger at Jacinta, the Visitor let out a deafening roar and swiped one of his great meaty arms sideways, straight into Alejandra. The little brunette girl flew straight into the lounge room wall and slid down, crumpling into an unmoving heap.

"No!!!" Jacinta cried and fired every round she had at the Visitor, who took each hit easily and simply regenerated itself.

Jacinta saw no way out and thought back to the ridiculous story Victoria had told her earlier when she and Ian had been held captive by the Visitor. Victoria had been right when she had said that there was no killing the Visitor unless something dead got a hold of it first.

Screams filled the void above her, and Jacinta knew it was Diana and Jose. As the Visitor drew closer to her, Jacinta kept pulling her trigger to nothing but the clicking sound of an empty chamber. She had left all of her weapons upstairs and had nothing left to fight the Visitor off with besides her empty gun. Drawing close enough to do so, Jacinta felt the Visitor's heavy metallic breathing as it gaped at her angrily. Almost fainting from the smell, Jacinta instead grabbed the butt of the gun and started pummelling the Visitor's head with its steely hammer.

The Visitor reared backward in pain, taking the gun with it, and Jacinta saw a caved-in area around its dark eyes. Green and purple ooze was covering the wound, and the Visitor apparently had sustained quite a bit of damage.

Taking a chance, Jacinta raced across the room to the body of Alejandra and checked her pulse points. It was then that Jacinta noticed the dark stain of blood mottled in with the girl's long brown hair.

The Visitor was stumbling back and forth with its back to her, temporarily blind from the wound Jacinta had inflicted. It suddenly turned back in her direction, and she saw the clear slime taking over the area and filling in the concaved mess that was the Visitor's eye.

Thinking fast, Jacinta lay down against the wall and pulled the still warm body of the deceased Alejandra on top of her. Jacinta concentrated on slowing her heart rate down from her adrenaline spike and held her breath. The Visitor screeched and looked around with it's now fully healed eye, but was unable to detect Jacinta's life force under Alejandra's dead body. She was still radiating heat, which mixed with Jacinta's underneath her, and rendered Jacinta nearly invisible to the once blinded Visitor.

The Visitor let out a mournful cry and took three strides with its long legs over to the broken window. It leaped out onto the edge of the balcony and disappeared from view as it climbed down the apartment building. Lying still, Jacinta watched as the other two Visitors descended down the apartment floors after it, passing quickly into view as it cleared the third level.

Jacinta quietly removed herself from underneath Alejandra's dead body and looked down into her motionless eyes—the colours fading as she searched for any last ray of hope. The electric blue colour that had rimmed her hypnotized eyes faded into brown and Jacinta knew there was nothing. She used her right hand to close Alejandra's eyes and whispered her apologies for not being able to get to her in time.

Getting up and making her way back into the main hall of the third floor, Jacinta broke into a sprint. She could feel her heartbeat rising again as she flew through the door to the stairwell that she had kicked open and leapt up the flights of stairs she had just run down.

Getting to the sixth floor, Jacinta ran straight down the corridor to where she had last seen Diana and Jose in the kitchen. She cried out for them, wishing to hear Diana speak in her native language but heard nothing but the whistling of the wind and the sound of the battle being waged outside at the Visitor's ship.

Rounding into the central area of the sixth floor, Jacinta stopped in her tracks. The window to the balcony had been broken, and shards of glass littered the grey carpet. Diana was lying face down on the kitchen floor; blood pooling underneath her face, her eyes glassy and her arms outstretched, reaching for her son. Jose's body was a little bit closer to the window than hers was, so the Visitors had obviously tried to take him when Diana intervened with a large metal pan that was lying next to her and covered in green and purple slime. Jose was not as lucky. His small body had been crumpled underfoot, and he lay crushed with concave areas on his upper back and legs.

Jacinta could barely look at them. She had been charged with protecting this family, trying to be the survivor and not going into battle. She had survived all right, but at the cost of everybody else.

The way that Jacinta saw it was that she had two options; she could take whatever she needed and run and leave the end-of-the-world heroics to the ones already out there, or she could get out there herself and prove that she was part of the group, and that the deaths of Diana, Alejandra and Jose were not in vein. Deciding quickly, Jacinta headed back to her bedroom and started gathering what she needed.

CHAPTER 10

Fast approaching the Visitor's ship in the middle of the intersection, Max, and Victoria knew they were going to have to get off their ride. Seeing a large empty grocery delivery truck in the middle of the road, Victoria saw her chance and swung her right leg over the bike so that she was sitting side-saddle. She kissed Max lightly on the cheek as he slowed the bike slightly and she jumped off, rolling along the concrete, feeling the gravel rash on her lower back and arm open up again despite the protection of her strong leather jacket.

Once the world stopped spinning, Victoria jumped to her feet and took off the across the short distance towards the delivery truck. She could hear the Mindless close behind her, and she jumped and climbed the ladder to the top of the truck as fast as she could.

At the top, Victoria crouched down low and felt the truck being jostled slightly as the Mindless continued to run after Max and the bike. She felt a few thuds and pounds and groans at the back of the truck, and she knew she had been spotted by a few of them when she had climbed to the top of the truck. There was no panic, though, as she could handle a few of them.

Victoria commando-crawled her way to the front of the truck and looked out across the scene ahead of her. The Visitors were aware of the sudden Mindless mob and were coming out of their ship with their laser cuffs at the ready. She saw Max slow down slightly, set the bike up and jump off only a few hundred meters from the ship—which was the closest anyone had managed.

Max barrel-rolled out of the way and took off behind another truck and SUV that were parked nearby. A couple of the Mindless followed him in pursuit, but the rest followed the deafening roar of the motorcycle as it crashed straight into the side of an upturned car lying crushed about fifty feet from the Visitor's ship, half-melted from its initial landing firestorm.

Suddenly a high pitched wailing noise sounded from inside the Visitor's ship, and all of the Visitors who had assembled in front of it turned and looked before turning back and crouched down low on their large ropey muscles of legs, poised for a fight.

Victoria heard the distant rumblings and shrieking's of the Mindless from the side of the mall and knew that Jay and Danny were closing in with the Mindless horde that they had gathered. She turned her head to the right and saw another horde running towards the ship from the high school where Mia and Hulio had just been. The plan was   coming together.

The Mindless that Max and Victoria had rounded up and led from the gym reached the ship, and the Visitors jumped from their battle stations. The air was filled with pulsating frequencies and blue energy blasts as the Visitors took out the Mindless with their high tech weaponry. Dust and debris billowed up in clouds around them blocking her view when suddenly Victoria heard the same ear-piercing shrill that had knocked her out of her daze when the Visitor had been attacked by one of the Mindless.

Straining to see through the dust, she scanned the scene and saw a Visitor flinging three or four Mindless creatures around like they were ragdolls as they bit and clawed their way into its body. It shrieked again as it was overrun and fell to the ground where it was suddenly silent amongst the flurry of motion from the Mindless. Victoria continued to scan the battle and saw several of the Visitors succumbing to the same vicious attacks at the clawing, decaying hands of the Mindless.

Blue electric gun blasts filled the air as other Visitors tried to save their fallen comrades, but to no avail. But no hesitation was given or remorse was shown when the Visitors who had been bit-ten started twitching and changing, and their fellow Visitors killed them mercilessly with their laser guns.

A few changed Visitors managed to escape through the sudden genocide and started attacking their own kind, which was the only creatures on the battlefield with a pulse. The Visitors in a Mindless state were even more ruthless and powerful than the typical Mindless were, and Victoria watched in mixed horror and fascination as a changed Visitor jumped onto the shoulders of another Visitor and twisted its head clean off, diving for its insides through the hole in its neck before the creature had a chance to heal itself. Another changed Visitor took off towards the SUV and the truck that Max had run behind, and Victoria knew it was time to get amongst the action.

Victoria jumped up and walked quickly across the steel roof to the back of the truck. She looked down directly into the red-rimmed eyes of three of the Mindless from the gym, still dressed in their gym clothes. She aimed her pistol directly into their heads and let off a round each, nailing them directly through their foreheads and lodging the bullets straight in their unthinking brains. The three thumped to the ground, and Victoria climbed down the ladder, taking off in Max's direction.

Now in the thick of the battle, Victoria jumped over charred Visitor bodies that the unchanged Visitors had disposed of. She ran around arms and legs that had been ripped from the attacking Mindless and avoided slipping in the large pools of congealing blood and flesh that dotted the concrete of the intersection. She tried to stay as well covered as possible, dodging the beams of the Visitor's electric blue rays, as she ran around the back of the truck on the other side to where Max had run. Looking around frantically, Victoria saw no sign of her husband.

Suddenly, a Mindless Visitor jumped down from the truck behind her and let out a terrifying sound that was a mixture of a gurgling snarl and an ear-piercing shriek. Victoria's eyes widened in surprise as she jumped backward. The Mindless Visitor reared itself towards her and Victoria quickly pulled the chainsaw from her back, pulling the ignition cord in a well-practiced motion. As the Mindless Visitor approached her in three fast bounds, Victoria aimed and let the rotating blade of the chainsaw rip straight through its neck. Her eyes widened in shock and terror as the blade lodged itself in the Visitor's thick neck, about four centimetres in, and whirred itself to a stop.

Letting out a curse, the air was suddenly filled with a shrill yell as the Mindless Visitor arched itself backward and started thrashing around in pain. Knowing she didn't have long until it launched its rage and pain at her, Victoria pulled her knife from the sheath on her belt and drove it forward, aimed at the creature's face. The Mindless Visitor turned its red-rimmed gaze straight at Victoria's blade as it closed in.

Green brain matter shot out and splattered Victoria as the Mindless Visitor thrashed and screamed, quickly falling with a dull thud on the cement. Victoria could hardly believe that she had brought one down.

Carefully walking towards the unmoving mass, Victoria put one steel capped boot on its shoulder and placed her hands on the handle of her chainsaw, still buried in the creature's neck. Breathing in slowly, she used all of her strength to try and pull the chainsaw out of the Mindless Visitor's ropey neck muscles. It wouldn't budge.

She tried a couple more times, but with the blades firmly latched in the Visitor's neck, there was nothing she could do but bid farewell to her favourite weapon. She grabbed the handle of her knife and dislodged it from the Visitor's bleeding eye socket before she reached down to take the cuff that clung to its wrist.

Victoria slowly picked up the Visitors arm and was surprised at how cold and clammy it felt. She held the arm up, struggling under the surprisingly heavy weight of it, and clicked a button on the underside of the cuff to release it from the wrist. It fell to the cement with a metallic clang, and she dropped the arm with a thud to retrieve the cuff.

Clicking a button that she hoped was the on switch, the cuff started to hum and vibrate slightly in her hand. Victoria could practically feel the other-worldly power springing from it and was momentarily distracted, getting used to the feel of this new weapon.

A loud explosion rattled overhead, on the other side of the truck that Victoria had been hiding behind. It jolted her mind back into the present. No matter what, she had to get to Max now!

Turning around, Victoria took off towards a bank of buildings that were situated next to the park opposite the mall. She covered the ground quickly, dodging a few dead bodies and debris that were being flung from the battle explosions behind her. She rounded the corner of a white building and was met with a terrifying sight. Max was standing on top of a car that had crashed through the park's boom gates in the original outbreak. He had his pistol out, shooting at a group of Mindless in front of him that were fast approaching the car, but he was quickly running out of bullets for the large group. Behind him, two Visitors were thrashing on the ground, changing into Mindless after being attacked by the horde now focused on Max.

At the back of the group, Victoria was unseen. She breathed in slowly and looked down at the cuff. Her vision swam in front of her as she remembered the buttons that the Visitor had pressed to shoot the one that had taken her and Ian. She pointed the cuff straight in front of her, aiming at the Mindless group, and pressed the array of buttons that she could remember.

The long metallic gun descended from its compartment on the cuff quickly and shot out straight in front of it. Victoria pressed one of the buttons and a blinding flash of blue electricity buzzed out of the barrel of the gun. The cuff had a powerful kick to its shot, and Victoria was forced backward slightly under the sudden pressure. She could feel every strand of hair on her body stand on end with the shot, but she hardly cared as she watched the first Mindless she had aimed for implode. Its congealing matter oozing from every orifice and falling to the ground.

Victoria pointed the cuff at the next closest Mindless and set off another zap of electricity. One after another she fired until she felt that her hair was standing on end like the Bride of Frankenstein. Victoria walked closer and closer to the horde as she fired, and bits of brain, blood, bone and flesh simply tore themselves away in an explosion of brilliant blue electricity. Pieces of the Mindless fell everywhere, and bodies lay unmoving on the ground.

Meanwhile, Max had heard the shrill awakening sound of the Mindless Visitors behind him. He had turned his back on the approaching horde when he saw Victoria approach with the cuff and started shooting at the Mindless Visitors numerous times, but finally, the hollow clicking sound indicated his pistol was empty. Max searched for more rounds but found none. Empty handed, he threw his empty gun down and pulled his knife from its stow in his boots just as one of the Mindless Visitors pounced on top of him.

Already weak from the fight, Max's mind raced to Victoria as he gruntingly let out a goodbye. Now crushed against the roof of the car, Max used all the power left in his arms and legs to push back against the Mindless Visitor, whose large cranium strained towards him. Its beady nostrils flared, taking in his living scent, and its red-rimmed eyes glowered in the near darkness of the smoky battlefield.

Suddenly the Mindless Visitor was stunned into stillness, and Max saw its eyes widen even more as blue electricity flashed through it. Green ooze started to slide out of its black eyes, enlarged nostrils and muzzle-like mouth, its head bursting suddenly before its body finally fell forwards onto Max, ten times heavier in death than in life.

Max struggled to breathe with the body of the heavy Mindless Visitor on top of him, and he strained his face away as he could feel the green ooze inside its body flow onto him. With his eyes slammed shut, the pink colouring behind his eyelids was infiltrated by another bright blue flash of electricity, and he could hear a wet thudding sound nearby.

With all of his might, Max pushed the weighted dead body of the Mindless Visitor off him, the body sliding in its own juices off the roof of the car, landing heavily on the grass below.

Max sat up on the roof, looking straight into the eyes of his wife. She was splattered lightly in purple blood and green brain matter, her brown hair standing on end and she was holding a long metallic gun, but Max thought he had never seen her looking more beautiful, nor been happier to see her alive and well. He knew his face was covered in the same green ooze that had seeped out of the Mindless Visitor, and with a quick wipe he slid off the car roof and pulled Victoria to him. They kissed, leaning on the blood-splattered car and surrounded by dead bodies.

Pulling away from the embrace, Victoria knelt down to face the body of the Mindless Visitor that had been on top of Max and clicked the button on the underside of the cuff to release it from the previous owner's wrist. She gave it to Max and quickly told him which buttons would operate the gun hidden within it before she ran around to the body of the other Mindless Visitor and removed its cuff as well.

"Let's get some more of these and get them to the others," Victoria told him, looking Max straight in the eyes. "With these, we will be unstoppable."

CHAPTER 11

Victoria and Max, now reunited but still in the heat of the battle, took off across the park to try and find the group. After luring the Mindless to the Visitor's ship to attack and turn all of the Visitors, the group had agreed to meet up in a small park next to the lake that was across from the mall. It was just far enough away from the battlefield to spring back into the action when the Mindless Visitors started to outnumber the Visitors and the Mindless.

Victoria and Max weaved their way through the debris, trying not to kill any Mindless they encountered to give them more time to turn as many Visitors as they could. Victoria had figured out that as normal Visitors they would constantly regenerate and heal themselves despite the pain inflicted on them, but after being bitten by the Mindless, they were left with the same curse of being dead, no longer being able to use their other-worldly senses to heal themselves. They could then be killed in the same way as the human Mindless, which was with major damage to the brain.

It also helped that the Visitors had a wonderful Mindless killing machine attached to their wrists that were guaranteed to work every time. If the group could steal sufficient numbers of them, there would be less up close and personal encounters with the Visitors from another world, not to mention the Mindless that had plagued their Earth.

Running across the park, Victoria looked out to the end of the road and saw Jay and Danny standing on a park bench that was perched on a grassy embankment next to the water. Danny was the first to spot them and started waving.

"Over here!" he cried out, as Jay pulled up a rifle and shot a Mindless that had been following them on their retreat. Almost reaching the end of the street, Victoria saw a series of Mindless bodies strewn around the littered road debris. It seemed that Jay and Danny had been there a while, setting up the meeting point to be as safe as possible. Victoria and Max ran straight to them as Danny became more and more obviously excited, bouncing up and down at their arrival.

"You made it! We made it!" He excitedly cried, as Victoria and Max stopped to catch their breath.

"Any sign of Hulio and Mia?" Victoria asked, ignoring Danny's optimism.

"No sign yet. They should be here soon … hopefully," Jay said as he put his rifle down, still scouting for them.

"Here guys, we got the guns," Victoria said as she pulled out the spare cuff she stole from the body of the Visitor she had shot down when one was attacking Max. "I've only got one spare at the moment, so whoever gets it has to kill another one, and we will collect them. It's surprisingly pretty easy to use …"

Victoria started showing the boys how to use the cuff, and they huddled around her next to the park bench while   Max looked out across the battlefield as a scout. He looked up quickly when he heard a sound to his left and saw Mia and Hulio running towards them, with a trail of Mindless behind them that they hadn't been able to shake.

"Guys!" Max cried and pulled out his cuff, clicking the series of buttons to turn it into a gun. Mia was in front, running as fast as she could and stained completely in dark purplish-red blood.

Hulio was panting behind her, a little too old to keep up after all they had already done.

Mia waved her arms at them and cried out as Max took aim, firing each bolt of electricity straight into the heads of the Mindless that were following them. The electric current sent a bolt of static energy into Max but forced the heads of the Mindless to implode and cave in on themselves, splattering in several different pieces along the road.

Victoria and Jay flicked their own cuffs into weapons and turned to the horde that was following them. Hulio struggled to breathe as he ran, slowing with every step while still trying to press on. Three of the Mindless in the group ran directly behind him and Victoria, Jay, and Max were unable to take them out without hitting Hulio first.

Mia slowed down as she approached the group, panting from her run. She turned to Hulio and called out to him to run faster. Hulio could barely breathe, and they all saw the look on his face, it was strained, bright red and sweaty from all the running, but the real look of horror was in his eyes. The whites had dulled to a gray color and they were bloodshot and reflecting the pain he held within.

It was his look of wanting to give up; the look of imminent death.

Mia, Jay, and Danny were all yelling at him to move faster, run faster and to get out of the way so that Victoria and Max could have a clear shot. The Mindless ran full of adrenaline as Max shot electricity bolts as close as possible to deter them. Victoria had started running in a wide arc to the right around the grassy embankment by the water to try and get a better angle, but it was too late.

Hulio collapsed under his own weight, with his legs buckling under him, exhausted. He landed on the cement, scraping his hands and tearing holes in the knees of his blood-stained jeans.

The Mindless were on top of him within seconds and ripping into his back. Hulio and Mia let out similar screams.

Max worked quickly and took out all three of the Mindless that were on top of Hulio, now that he had a clear shot. One fell onto Hulio's body as he writhed in pain. Victoria ran forward in Hulio's direction from her side position, and Danny ran forward and held onto Mia by the waist as she doubled in anguish with her tears flowing freely.

In a few quick bounds, Victoria reached Hulio's body and pushed a Mindless with an oozing and concaved head off of him. The damage was extensive, with huge rips and tears into his skin on his back—blood pooling in the deep wounds. Victoria sat beside Hulio and pulled him to her knees, careful not to scrape the open wound on the concrete. Hulio looked up at Victoria and stuttered to say something in whispered Spanish that she couldn't understand.

"Shhh. Hulio, it's OK … Just Shhh …" she said as she stroked his dark sweat-matted hair. She felt Max approach quickly and stand behind her. Hulio's dull eyes blinked out at her from under his blood-caked face as he drew in his last breath. All the light that was left in his eyes quickly drained away, and Victoria was astonished as she saw his brown eyes begin to develop a ring of red around the irises almost immediately.

Hulio's battered body began to twitch and wriggle underneath her as his transformation into one of the Mindless began to take effect. She quickly and quietly pulled his head off her lap and onto the concrete before standing up next to Max, who was pointing Jay's pistol at his head.

"I'm sorry," Max whispered to their friend before he pressed the button on the gun, causing Hulio's body to stop twitching. They turned away as his fresh blood and brain matter began to leak onto the concrete.

*****

They waited half an hour by the lake, resting and preparing for the next stage in their battle plan—thinking about Hulio but trying not to dwell on his death. They took it in turns to patrol the area and kill off any Mindless or Mindless Visitors that approached, but the majority of the fight continued to reign on around the Visitor's ship. Explosions rocked Mia out of her broken sleep, exhausted from crying after seeing her partner in the fight fall.

Victoria watched the battle through the scope of a rifle, with Max searching out straggling Mindless around them. The Mindless were winning because they outnumbered the Visitors five to one. They attacked mercilessly and ceaselessly and fell only when a Visitor got to their weaponised cuffs in time. For the most part, the Visitors were overcome and attacked, completely eaten in a spray of purple blood and green brain matter, or bitten badly enough to turn into one of them once the Mindless were thwarted in their attacks.

Bodies lay everywhere, squashed and decaying human heads that belonged to the Mindless with brain matter and debris seeping out of them, as well as the strong gray arms of the Visitors lying twitching in heaps, trying to regrow onto partially devoured bodies. The Visitor's ship had opened, and it seemed that the entire invasion had flooded out onto the battlefield to stem the attack from the Mindless.

Some of the Mindless had managed to get up the ramp of the Visitor's ship and go inside. The small group could hear the sound of explosions and dying shrieks coming from within, and shortly afterward a large group of Mindless Visitors emerged to attack its comrades that had not fallen already. Slowly, the Visitors were all being turned into stronger, more agile killing machines.

"Alright guys," Victoria said, taking her sights out of the rifle and pushing off the bench. "I think it's time we get back in there. It looks like the majority of the Visitors have been turned into Mindless and to stop them from getting too far from the battlefield and into the city, we need to attack them now.”

Mia pulled herself up from her lying position, resting on Danny who was helped to his feet. Jay joined them from his post by the lake.

“Everyone knows the drill. Danny and Mia go with Jay and get one of the weapons from a fallen Visitor. Use it on everyone and everything that isn’t one of us,” Max continued the speech, “Kill the Mindless and kill the Mindless Visitors. The more we take out, the better our chances are going to be. We don’t leave the battlefield until none of them are left standing.”

“Or none of us are left standing,” Mia said bitterly. They all looked at each other in the circle: a married couple, a young girl and two weedy had-been stoners. It was an odd group, but it was a family, and they needed one after all they had lost.

“I love you guys,” Jay told the group, and they all murmured their loving replies. They quickly hugged and looked to Max, who nodded at them all.

In one fluid motion, the group took off running into the battlefield; ready to fight to the death for the survival not only of themselves but of what was left of humankind.   Victoria and Max went running towards the park to arc around the left-hand side of the Visitor’s ship, while Jay, Danny, and Mia took off to the right. Rested now, Mia easily kept up with the running speed of her tall and lanky friends, despite their larger gait. They ducked through the side of the mall and ran through a car park that was full of abandoned vehicles, trying to avoid the edge of the ship as much as possible. Their plan was to corner one of the Mindless Visitors and grab its cuff so they could build their defences and weaponry.

Hiding behind a large concrete pillar at the edge of the car park, Jay peeked out to try and spot a Mindless Visitor and heard a commotion in a nearby café on the other side of the street. He could just make out the large mottled body of a Visitor through the glass, and he pointed towards the store to communicate to Danny and Mia where they were going.

Between the pillars they were hiding behind and the store, were six of the Mindless in tattered and blood-soaked clothes, now wandering aimlessly along the street. Danny flicked back the hammer on his sawn-off shotgun and Mia pulled her knife out and held it, tightly gripped in her hand, ready to strike.

Jay counted down silently from three using his fingers and when they hit one all three of them took off across the street. Jay fired his Visitor gun at one of the Mindless with long curly brown hair while Danny shot a blonde teenage girl straight through the head. Mia followed closely behind, taking up the rear but not being in close enough range to do any permanent damage with her knife. Around her, the Mindless fell to Jay and Danny's long range weapons as they crossed the street, but something she saw up the road traveling away from the Visitor's ship made her stop in her tracks.

It was Beth, who had travelled with the horde from the school and hadn't attacked the Visitors. She was just standing in the middle of the road, covered in dried blood and an eerie look of defiance on her face.

When Mia and Hulio had raced through the high school with her Mindless classmates on their tails, Mia hadn't had a chance to stop and free Beth from her undead doom. Mia had actually pushed Beth out of the way and into one of the school bushes as she was running past her to avoid having Beth swept up in the Mindless horde destined for battle. She had plans to return to the school and retrieve her and give Beth the proper burial she deserved.

Now, Mia and Beth stood in the middle of the road, meters apart and in the midst of a battlefield like two Western gunslingers. Jay and Danny had kept up their sustained attack on the rest of the Mindless in the street, and then continued into the café as they had planned, unaware that Mia was not following them. Time seemed to stand still for a moment, and Mia was unaware of anything else but her ragged breathing and her vision of Beth, who locked her red-rimmed eyes with Mia's blue ones. Beth suddenly started sprinting towards her and Mia found herself racing to meet her friend in the middle of the street.

With an angry growl, Beth leaped towards her and Mia forced herself into a stop and steeled herself for the attack. She pulled the arm holding the knife backward and lunged it straight forward with all of her strength, letting out an exasperated yell. The blade struck straight between Beth's red-rimmed eyes. With an angry gurgling sound, the momentum of Beth's run forced her head to slide forward into the knife and hang, lightly growling, from Mia's strong outstretched arm still holding the knife.

Realizing what had happened, Mia let out a frightened gasp and let go of her grip on the knife, sending Beth's body falling to the ground with a heavy thud. Mia swallowed back tears as she looked down at her friend's body lying broken and decaying on the ground.

Suddenly, Mia was hit from the right with a terrifying force that knocked her to the ground. Gravel embedded itself into her soft flesh and her vision filled with twinkling stars as she knocked her temple heavily on the cement.   Through the blurring black vision, she opened her eyes in a dazed motion and was met with the empty black and red-rimmed eyes of a Mindless Visitor. It had barrelled on top of her in its attack and was now screaming and shrieking at her, ready to bite into her shoulder and turn Mia into one of them.

As Mia's vision swam, all she could think about was that she was glad that Beth had finally been put to rest. She put her throbbing head back down to the cool concrete and awaited the end. She was almost happy to be out of the terror that plagued her everyday life and felt a longing to no longer feel the pain and anguish that darkened her world.

In an instant, the pressure on the Mindless Visitor pinning her to the ground was released as the creature was knocked on its side. With the sudden release of pressure, Mia tried to drag her mind back from the brink of unconsciousness and forced her eyes open to see Jacinta running in from behind her, hacking into the Mindless Visitor with a long sword. It thrashed and it's muzzle like mouth made shrieking motions Mia couldn't hear while trying to get up, but Jacinta put all of her strength and drive into each blow, severing arms and stabbing its torso before driving the blade straight through the Visitor's oversized cranium.

Mia's vision continued to swim in and out of a deep well of blackness and she found she had very little power of her own at the moment. Jacinta approached her, covered in spots of blood that was brilliantly coloured in red, purple and green—a gruesome mix of both human blood and of Visitor blood and brain. She mouthed words to Mia, but Mia couldn't hear anything but a loud buzzing noise.

Jacinta pulled Mia to her feet and put her arms around her, pushing her forward and out of the street. Jacinta had heard loud yells and cries coming from the shop so she approached it with caution. Supporting a weak Mia, Jacinta managed to carefully climb through the broken window at the front of the shop.

Among up-turned tables and chairs, Jay was lying half-conscious near the entrance, looking battered and bruised. The large Mindless Visitor was feverously working with its back to the girls. Unaware of what was going on, Jacinta let go of Mia and readied her sword, approaching the Mindless Visitor. Through her swimming vision, Mia saw the Visitor's cuff that Jay had been holding lying on the floor across the coffee shop and she stumbled towards it.

Jacinta quietly approached the Mindless Visitor, and just centimetres from its body, she inadvertently stood on a broken ceramic mug that made a loud crunching noise under her boot.

Her eyes widened as the Mindless Visitor turned towards her and she fully grasped the situation.

The Visitor's suction cupped hands and dark muzzle-like mouth were covered in blood, and a loose trail of flesh and cloth was hanging out of its mouth like a strand of spaghetti. Behind it lay Danny, dead and sprawled out on the ground with his face stuck in a permanent state of shock and terror. His body's cavity lay open with fresh ribs sticking out at odd angles and his insides torn apart in a bloody mess. Seeing the state of Danny caused Jacinta to momentarily hesitate in shock before beginning to strike the Mindless Visitor, and it gave the creature just enough time to back-hand Jacinta with a swipe of its strong muscled arm. Jacinta hit her head hard against the wall and crumpled to the ground motionless, while the Mindless Visitor turned back to its meal.

Mia stumbled and reached for the cuff lying on the ground, hitting the on buttons that Victoria had shown her. She stood up from her crouched position, wobbled a bit as her vision came in waves, and aimed the gun at the Mindless Visitor, who, now alerted to her presence, had turned towards her.

"Get off of my planet," Mia snarled and pressed the button. The gun whirred into life and sent a shock of electricity straight into the Mindless Visitor. Its gray cranium caved in under the assault of the electricity and green brain matter began to splatter and ooze from its head. The Mindless Visitor let out a howling shriek that pierced the buzzing noise in Mia's head before it fell lifeless to the floor. The electric shock from the gun pressed into Mia's throbbing temples, and she felt the blackness close in around her as she followed it, falling to the ground.

Coming in and out of the darkness, Mia was vaguely aware that Jay had awoken and was yelling loudly. She watched through the pulsing strobe light of her vision as Jay crossed the floor of the coffee shop towards his fallen best friend.

Suddenly, everything went black.

CHAPTER 12

Jay screamed and cursed for the loss of his friend, kneeling next to what remained of Danny's body. His painful cries were loud enough to rouse Jacinta from where she lay crumpled against the wall. She quickly sprang up and took in the scene, only relaxing when she saw the oozing head of the Mindless Visitor next to Jay and Danny.

Jacinta pulled Jay to his feet and snapped some sense into him. "Jay, stop it," she yelled heartlessly. "Whining won't bring him back. Get revenge on them. It's the only way we're going to win this war."

Jay nodded, trying to pull himself together. He turned to the body of the Mindless Visitor that had killed his best friend and leaned down to undo the cuff on its wrist. He quickly showed Jacinta how to use it, and she went off to try and wake Mia. Jay let his anger out by kicking the body of the Mindless Visitor several times until purple blood and gray flesh covered the tips of his boots.

He screamed at it once more with his full lung power, and with one last look over at his friend, forced himself away to help Jacinta lift Mia up. She would not wake from her fall but was still alive and breathing, so together they pulled her into the back office of the café and locked the door behind them.

Leaving Mia safe for the moment and heading back to the battlefield, and Jay, spurred on by a need for revenge, let loose against the Mindless Visitors. With a newfound sense of urgency and anger, he didn't hesitate to wipe them out, one after another, shooting the electric power of the gun into their enlarged craniums. Mercilessly, and without stopping, Jay and Jacinta obliterated every last walking Mindless and every last hungry Mindless Visitor that they came across.

Moving among the debris of the street, the battle had finally quietened. Jay and Jacinta walked slowly and purposefully, with Jay firing sprays of the blue electricity into the heads and bodies of even the motionless and dead Mindless Visitors. There was no end to the sorrow of losing his best friend, the only person he had been close to. And in his rage, there was no end to the shooting, even if what he was shooting was already permanently dead.

Picking through the battle's remains, Jacinta and Jay came across Victoria and Max, who were covered in blood but had successfully obliterated the last of the Mindless Visitors on their side of the battle. They had searched the dead bodies and had started collecting all remaining cuffs off the bodies. Approaching Jacinta and Jay, Victoria and Max were suddenly weary.

"Jacinta? What are you doing here?" Victoria asked. "What happened to staying behind to protect Diana, Alejandra, and Jose?"

"Where's Hulio?" Jacinta answered, skirting the topic.

"He's dead. The Mindless got him. We tried to save him but something in him … it let go," Victoria answered, haunted by the sight of her deceased friend.

"Well, at least he's with his family now," Jacinta nonchalantly answered Victoria's original question.

"They're dead?" Victoria gasped, looking at Jacinta in disbelief.

"   You know only the strong survive," Jacinta said finally. Behind her, Jay let off another stream of brilliant blue sparks into a Mindless Visitor's dead body, letting out a stream of curses in answer to Jacinta's statement.

"Danny and Mia?" Max asked, interrupting the catfight that was about to break out.

"Mia's fine. She got knocked out, and we've locked her in a back office in the café, so she's safe." Jacinta answered, looking directly at him and avoiding Victoria's deadly glares that she was shooting at her.

"Danny's gone …" Jay piped up, hardly able to choke out the words. "He's freaking gone …." Jay dropped his cuff and fell to his knees with his eyes to the ground. His hands reached up to cover his face as fresh tears stung his eyes. Victoria walked over to Jay and knelt next to him, but he waved her away, wanting no comfort in his grief.

"Well Miss Smarty Pants, tell me," Jacinta gritted her teeth and turned towards Victoria, "What do we do about the ship huh? Do you want to go in there and see if they're all dead?"

Victoria looked towards the entrance ramp of the ship, which was covered in metal and stuck out past the ship's metal tubing that covered its surface. She wondered what was left in there.

"Blow it," Jay said from beneath his hands. The group turned towards him, questioning, and he looked up at them. "Blow it up. Blow every last piece to kingdom come. It will kill everything inside, and we won't get any more nasty surprises."

"And how do we do that Jay? Got any dynamite on you?" Jacinta asked bitterly, spitting out the question.

"You don't need dynamite," Jay rose from his feet with a determined look on his face. "Danny told me about this one time, that one of his friends stole a car and used it for target practice. He said he accidentally shot one of the gas cylinders, and the whole thing blew up. I reckon that's what these pipes are for that are all around the ship. I reckon if we all shoot at it in different areas, we could blow it up."

"What if that doesn't work?" Jacinta demanded.

"So what? At least we tried, and the worst case scenario is that we have to go in there and face it. I'd rather not do that first if an explosion would work," Jay answered.

"We just need enough firepower to start an explosion," Victoria said, suddenly having light bulbs going off in her brain. "And I know just where to get it!"

Upon hearing Victoria's quick explanation of her revelation, the group split up. Victoria and Max ran to the army vehicle that had been lying next to the overturned SUV that Victoria had hidden in when the Visitor had tried to take her and Ian. When they reached it, they started a methodical search, trying to find any of military grade firepower that may have been hidden from looters in the area. Victoria searched the dead soldiers and came up with two grenades still attached to the front of their belts, thinking that they would do nicely.

Meanwhile, Jacinta and Jay went back down to the café to move Mia as far away from the Visitor's ship as possible. Luckily, Mia had awakened, albeit still dazed and confused, in the back office. The group then retrieved more guns from their supply at the apartments and met at the edge of the stairs where only a few days ago Victoria and Max had been running up trying to escape the Mindless that had chased them while on a supply run. It seemed like years ago now.

When the group met up, Victoria quickly squeezed Mia's shoulders as a sign of comfort to the young girl and showed the others what they had found. Jay and Max moved closer to the ship while the girls stayed behind and laid down on the concrete behind a large pillar, their army surplus rifles, and guns aimed at various pipes built around the outside of the ship. Jay and Max carefully walked through the debris one last time, approaching as close to the mouth of the ramp on the Visitor's ship as possible. They nodded in anticipation and steeled themselves.

Pulling the pins from the two grenades in unison, Jay and Max lobbed the small, heavy-duty explosives as hard and as a far as they could before turning and running for cover behind a tall pillar at an office block across the street from the apartments. As soon as Jay and Max started running, Mia, Victoria, and Jacinta all levelled their guns, firing directly into the series of pipes that surrounded the ship.

Just as Jay and Max reached the edge of the office building, the grenades exploded inside the Visitor's ship. The fire from the grenades ignited the inside of the ship and the whole side of it exploded in a brilliant ball of metal, sparkling blue electricity and fire. The wind from the explosion picked up and flew past the girls with the same intensity that the Visitor's ship had landed with. Victoria, Jacinta, and Mia all put their heads to the ground with their hands over their skulls to protect themselves as metallic debris and body parts came flying past them.

Jay and Max hid behind the concrete walls of the office building and Jay could hear the tinkling crashing sound of windows breaking all around them. Large fiery hunks of metal that resembled engines flew past them and on down the street with great velocity, and the ground itself seemed to shake with the explosion. Countless bodies of the Mindless and the Mindless Visitors alike were incinerated in the explosion, and those body parts not vaporised came raining down on the group as if they were in the middle of a raging storm.

The explosive fire raged on, burning some unknown oil and gas that leaked from the ship. In a while, when the explosion had died down and left a regular fire in its wake, Max and Jay stuck their heads around the block to inspect the damage. The ship was destroyed, leaving a mass of molten smouldering metal where it had stood. Metal and shards of glass were splayed everywhere across the intersection, and the corner of the mall closest to the ship was now on fire in a brilliant blaze.

Victoria, Jacinta, and Mia peeked up from beneath their hands before getting to their feet. Ash was floating down all around them and landing on the street like snow. They slowly walked to the middle of the road to meet Max and Jay, who were walking over from the other side of the street.

"Is it over?" Mia asked hesitantly, looking out at the destruction burning before them. Taking in the damage, Victoria sighed with relief and leaned on Max's broad shoulders.

"Yeah. I think it might be," Max answered her, a big smile broadening on his face as he leaned in to kiss his wife.

*****

After the fire had burnt itself out, and the group was certain that there were no Visitors remaining, they collected the members of their group who had perished in the battle. It was a grizzly process, and they tried to preserve the remains of the most violent deaths of Danny, Hulio and Jose in a series of white sheets they had used as bedding in what was once their home in the apartment block.

Max and Victoria dug six graves on the grassy embankment, one for each of them including Beth, who Mia insisted on giving a proper burial. It was a long process, but the bodies of their friends were soon interred in their graves.

Mia made six large crosses out of branches from a fallen tree and some rubbery twigs and buried their stems into the ground at the base of each of the graves. The group encircled the piles of dirt containing their friends and bowed their heads.

"We stand here today to commemorate the lives and deaths of our friends Danny, Hulio, Diana, Alejandra, Jose and Beth," Max began, speaking for the group. "They survived so much horror during this turbulent time, but now their horror has ended, and they are free to be at peace. We will miss you, good friends."

The group whispered words of love and sadness into the air, thinking of the good times they had enjoyed with their friends; trying not to think of the bad. After a minute of silence, they lifted their heads and began to turn away from the graves, walking back towards the apartment building and past the smoldering rubble of the Visitor's ship and the now burning mall.

"So what now?" Jacinta asked.

"Jacinta, we've all come to a decision, and it's not one that we made lightly," Victoria answered. "We're going to head west to try and find a new home for ourselves, one that's hopefully free of Mindless and Visitors." Victoria paused and then said, "We don't want you to come with us."

"Excuse me? After all, I've done for the group; you're going to kick me out now?" Jacinta cried, outraged at the group's decision. She stopped in her tracks, and the group stood around with her.

"We can't trust you, Jacinta. You wouldn't help us with the battle, and you didn't help Diana, Alejandra and Jose," Max chimed in, putting a protective arm around his wife's shoulders. "It has become apparent that you are only out to save yourself, and we feel that should the time come, you would sacrifice any member of this group to do so. We need to work together as a team, and we don't think you can."

"This is bull," Jacinta bit back, "I've saved many of your lives. I kept you Mia!" she turned towards the girl, looking small and frail wrapped in a blue woollen blanket to provide some comfort after her ordeal.

"Don't bring her into this, Jacinta!" Victoria cried at her, reaching out to pull Mia into her embrace. "We've all decided that your actions and your motives are unclear and that you've always done what's best for yourself, not what was best for the group. We want to try and start mankind again. We have the weapons and the technology now actually to defend ourselves."

"Don't be so naive Victoria; there is no starting humankind again. This is where the human race ends," Jacinta answered bitterly.

"No, it doesn't." Victoria declared, putting a hand lightly on her stomach, thinking back to the pregnancy test she had looted from the mall before the Visitor's fell from the sky. "I'm pregnant Jacinta. Life can go on."

Jacinta looked at Victoria's stomach in disbelief. "You're pregnant? Are you crazy?" she cried, "Bringing a child into this world is condemning it and everyone else to death!" She pulled her face closer to Victoria's, and Max stood to attention beside her. "When it cries, they will hear, and they will come looking for you. They will finish you off and pick your poor baby's bones clean."

"This is why we have to find somewhere safe to start again. This is why we don't want you with us," Victoria answered her, slow and calculated.

Jacinta pulled herself straight to reach her full height. She glared around, and each member of the group, and she read it in all of their faces except Mia's. They all believed Victoria, and they all refused to trust her.

"Fine," Jacinta finally said through gritted teeth. "I don't want to be around a crying baby anyway. It's going to be the death of you all."

"We would appreciate it if you went east," Victoria declared and gave her a hard look. Jacinta refused to say anything but simply watched as Victoria, Max and Jay turned their backs on her and started walking towards the apartment building again. Jacinta looked at Mia, still standing there with her big blue eyes widened.

After a moment, Mia walked up to Jacinta and pulled her hand out from under the blanket wrapped around her, grabbing Jacinta's own hand. Startled by the sudden display of affection, Jacinta could only look at her in surprise.

"Thank you, Jacinta," Mia finally spoke in a kind tone. "Thank you for saving me, and thank you for what you've done for us. I'm sorry it has to be like this."

With that, Mia let go of Jacinta's hand, leaving something cold and heavy in her palm. She wrapped her hand back under the blanket draped around her shoulders and followed after Victoria, Max and Jay.

Jacinta looked down at the Visitor's metal cuff that Mia had given her. It was cold and lifeless in her hand, but she could feel the energy buzzing off it. Jacinta looked up and watched them leave. The group headed back to the apartment to collect what little food, water and possessions they had before they set out to find a new world.

Maybe they could make it, she thought. Maybe they would find the perfect corner of the sky that was safe from Visitors and safe from the Mindless. Maybe they could restart humanity among the decaying mass of death and debris and violence. Maybe they would all be alright, and maybe even she, Jacinta, would find her place in this frightening world. She had to hope that she would.

Because in the end, hope was all they had. Like a flame, lighting up the darkness, hope will only burn brighter the closer you got to it.

But once you got to the light, you'll see that it all had a meaning, and a reason behind it. You will see that it would all be worth it in the end.

It had to be.

EPILOGUE

Among the debris of the Visitor's ship, still smouldering lightly from the fire that had consumed it, a large gray heavily muscled arm lay severed from its body, just three steps away. The body was charred and burned in the explosion but lay in its viscous decay, cut raggedly through the abdomen. The Visitor's large head was damaged but still attached to the body, and its dark pit eyes were open but unseeing, the pain so intense that it burned with a white-hot flame.

The arm started twitching. Slowly and trifling at first, but soon the three suction-cupped fingers on the end of the hand began to move in a disjointed fashion. Clear mucus began to seep from the severed end of the arm, pulling it towards the body. It was unable to fully repair itself, based on the extent of damage done to the cranium of the Visitor, but the arm continued to twitch and creep towards its host.

Pulling into the socket, the clear mucus began to reattach and assemble itself to the upper torso of the Visitor. First came the reattachment of the overlarge and protruding metallic bones, then the massive hunk of muscle and tendon that roped together to bind the bones in place. Next, the blood began to flow up the disjointed fingers and into the chest cavity of the Visitor before some of it began to flow in a purple ooze out of the ripped and burning abdomen.

The blood filled what was left of the Visitor's oversized brain, and it was able to see again momentarily. Its field of vision was no longer white, but an almost blinding dark purple that fed images of rubble and death to the Visitor's mind. The Visitor moved what was left of its head stiffly and saw the ragged and charred destruction to its body. It tried to let out a shriek, but no noise came from its muzzle-like mouth.

The Visitor was in the control room of the ship, or at least what was left of it. Large oversized metallic panels ran across the bridge just above where the Visitor was lying. It looked out of the dark viewing windows above the panels and saw the only smoky gray sky above it.

Knowing it was the end, with what little strength it had, the Visitor twitched its now fully functioning arm. With one last surge of force, the Visitor flung the arm ungracefully above its head onto the control panels across the bridge where it had once sat with such pride and power.

The arm seemed to move and felt along the melted buttons until it came to a large metal switch that had been burnt beyond recognition. The Visitor forced itself, trying to focus behind the sudden flashes of white it was experiencing, to pry its suctioned fingers into the metal and pull. The metal came apart easily, destroyed by the flames, and the Visitor tossed it aside gently.

Dipping one of the suction cupped tips into the hole left by the discarded metal, the Visitor pressed down as hard and as far as it could. Its suction tips found the edge of a button, and it pressed with all the remaining strength it could muster.

With the switch engaged, above it, the Visitor could hear a slow whirring sound, followed by a faint beeping noise that was barely audible to its well-tuned vibration signals. Letting go, the Visitor's arm flopped down from the control panel to lie splayed out on the floor of the ship. The Visitor's world was filled with a white hot searing pain again that ripped it from life, and it let go to meet the end.

The faint beeping noise reacted like a pulse as it sent its signal out into the sky. It vibrated through the clouds, through the polluted atmosphere and into the dark abyss of space. It pulsed past twinkling stars and planets in their rotation around the sun, the noise continuing to reverberate into the darkness of space beyond the solar system.

Searching the dark recesses of space, the beeping pulse finally bounced off its target and met its intended purpose; warning another fleet of Visitor ships that were lying dormant beyond the galaxy, of the destruction and failure of their first scouting mission—the Visitors who had been sent in to clean up after the plague they had unleashed on Earth to cleanse it so many years ago. A Visitor stood behind a control panel similar to the one that the pulse had been sent from, and it bowed its large mottled cranium.

Understanding the signal's meaning, the Visitor turned to its fellow guardsmen and let out a long ear-piercing shriek.

The contamination process to inhabit the human's world had forced the strong to survive; the push to stop the destruction of their earth had required defensive action, and they had risen to it.

The Visitor turned back toward its panel in the control room, setting a course for the fleet to make the journey to the new world, to finish what they had started.

READ WHAT HAPPENS NEXT IN

Cosmic Decay: Debris

Out Now

Prologue

The road can be long and harsh, especially when left abandoned and met with solitude. Deserted cars were left to rust along silent highways, belongings scattered from the trunks, and long-congealed blood smeared on the cracked tarmac.

It had been more than five years since the end of the world. The concrete jungle had crumbled into ruin in a short amount of time and the Earth's population was decimated by a rage-fuelled virus that overtook the collective mind. Humans became the Mindless; scavengers filled with hunger, feasting on bloodlust and hate until it seeped into their bones and devoured them from the inside out. The decay and the rot spread, and all that was left was an empty abyss inside their minds — and outside in their world.

The Mindless roamed listlessly without a fresh supply of anger and blood to fuel their adrenaline. They congregated in cities and towns, stuck in a constant search for food, and when their meals ran out, they wandered and roamed further into the world looking for fresh flesh. But those who were unable to walk - who crawled and clawed their way across the ground - could not leave the places where they'd turned and so they slumped in dormant decay, doomed to be forever hungry.

These Mindless creatures were the product of an otherworldly virus, infected into the population with the intent of destroying it and returning the globe to a natural balance more suited for habitation by those of another world. The Earth was identified as an important and precious resource, and Visitors from this other world wanted to claim it as their own.

With the successful contamination of the human race, the Visitors rejoiced in the world that they were creating. Nature began to reclaim the manmade roads and infrastructures, devouring all in its path. Tree roots cracked the untended roads, and plants began to grow among the rubble. Left in complete freedom, nature took back what had been stolen from it as civilisation had ceased and the planet rejoiced in its renewal.

Animals were beginning to return to the less inhabited areas, though they were still few and far between. They were skittish, distrustful of these new versions of predators who smelled of blood and ripped into the flesh of unwary creatures. The animals of this Earth had learnt to be silent, to exercise their flight reflexes instead of their fight ones, and so they existed primarily unseen in the forests surrounding the decay.

The sun still rose and set with each day, and the seasons still came and went, but they began to return to a pre-climate change environment without man's interference of deforestation and pollution, and relentless advancement.

The Earth itself seemed to rejoice in this rejuvenation, and invited the Visitors in their claim on the jewelled planet. The Visitors had, after all, freed it from destruction.

But others living on the Earth were not so welcoming. Some resourceful humans had survived the contamination and had fought back against the virus, the invasion and then the initial settlement.

Their primitive minds had surprisingly laid the Visitors' plans to waste and caused the first settlers to fail in their duty to cleanse the contamination of Earth. The Visitors had spent years planning and arranging the tools and planting the virus among the human race that inhabited and ruled the planet, and had agreed that the first settlers would systematically remove the contamination – both the virus and any leftover humans. They would then claim the world, signalling to their brethren to join them and continue their dominion of this, their new realm.

The early settlers had not intended that the humans would have survived against their sophisticated and deadly bio-weapons, and had come unprepared for a fight. Distracted by their inflated egos, the Visitors had lost the battle for ownership of the Earth.

But they were determined they would not lose the war.

Across the gulf of space, a fleet of ships filled with Visitors awaited a signal from the first settlers, indicating the success of their mission and the start of a new life on Earth. But the beeping pulse received was actually the signal with a different meaning – a distress signal.

The initial settlement had failed.

The Commander of the Visitors – notable only by the small stripe of neon green light that glowed around the cold metallic cuff it wore on its right wrist – stood at attention behind a control panel. Large oversized metallic panels ran across the bridge and a dark viewing window in front of it opened out to the dark star-filled galaxy.

Positioned around the command room, Visitors usually swarmed around similar controls, moving back and forth on suction-cupped toes. But as the faint beeping reverberated around the metallic command room, they stood stock-still and listened to the last remaining voice of their comrades in arms.

The Commander turned to its fellow guardsmen and let out an ear-piercing shriek that filled the room and shook all from their stupor. They jumped to attention and rushed to their controls as the Commander angrily turned to its own and set a course for the fleet to journey to their new world.

This would not be the entrance they had imaged.

With all of their heavy machinery, weaponry and technological advancements, their superior intelligence and the element of surprise, the Visitors couldn't believe the humans had gotten the better of them and they refused to turn their backs on all they had worked so hard to take.

Their first fleet would not die in vain. This precious world would still be theirs.

ACKNOWLEDGEMENTS

Byron Carr - for not only supporting me throughout the entire process of this novel, but for designing an amazing front cover for it too.

Alison Lewis – A published author yourself, you are an inspiration to me.

Colin Lewis – Writing is clearly running through our genes, so thank you for helping to pass it to me.
Ben Lewis – You're absolutely the coolest person I know and one amazing big brother.

Marion Mapham – Without even knowing it you have done so much more for me than simply editing my work, so thank you so much for everything.

Nicole Powell – My best friend, thank you for sharing in all of celebrations and successes with me in the more than ten years I have had the joy of knowing you.

And to all of my other friends and family who have supported me and celebrated with me thank you so much for everything. I couldn't have done it without you!

ABOUT THE AUTHOR

Courtney Hope is an author from Canberra, Australia, writing for many different publications and blogs including her own event planning blog The Party Connection, and a horror pop culture blog called This Side of Sanguine.

She may look like a cupcake, but Courtney is wickedly dark, enjoying listening to rock music, drinking too much red wine, watching too many horror movies, and living an environmentally-friendly hygge lifestyle. She is a vegan, a dog owner, and a pop culture fan.

She has written a party planning handbook called *Secrets of a Party Planner*, as well as *Cosmic Decay: Contamination*. Her third novel in the series, *Cosmic Decay: Absolution* will be available in the future.

www.courtneyhope.com.au
www.thepartyconnectionaustralia.com
www.thissideofsanguine.com